Belle

Belle

BEVERLY JENKINS

KIMANI
TRU
™

Recycling programs
for this product may
not exist in your area.

BELLE

ISBN-13: 978-0-373-83133-3
ISBN-10:   0-373-83133-1

A Kimani TRU title published by Kimani Press/January 2009

First Published by Avon Books in 2002 as BELLE AND THE BEAU

www.KimaniTRU.com

Printed in U.S.A.

This book is dedicated to Carrie, Meredith, Alexandra and Sibhan—thanks ladies, for helping me get this right.

Thanks also to Abby for being a writer's dream.

one

April 1859
Whittaker, Michigan

SIXTEEN-year-old Belle Palmer's feet burned like they were on fire. She knew the pain came from all the walking she'd been doing in the too-large boots, and that the soles of her feet were probably raw and covered with blisters, but she couldn't stop and rest. It had now been five days since slave catchers had descended on their small party of Kentucky runaways, and Belle and her pa had been separated in the bedlam that followed as everyone ran for their lives. Five days of sleeping on the ground; five days of eating whatever she could find in the fields; and five days of being lost and alone. She'd come North looking for freedom and found only the freedom to starve. With no idea where she was or how to find someone she could trust, she had no choice but to keep moving. The White man who'd guided them into Michigan told them all what to look for should a disaster occur. Folks friendly to escaped slaves hung colored quilts out on their clotheslines; other houses had little Black-faced jockeys out front, and if the lantern in the jockey's hand was lit, it meant fugitives were welcomed. Belle had passed many farmhouses but had seen no such signs.

She'd also committed to memory the secret phrases Underground Railroad conductors sometimes asked to determine if a runaway was indeed who they claimed to be. She remembered all the corresponding answers but couldn't find anyone to ask her the questions.

The early April weather had turned colder last night. She pulled her threadbare coat tighter and forced back the tears filling her eyes from the agony in her feet. Her ugly, homespun trousers were no match for the Michigan chill and she shivered in the gray dawn air. She thought about home and what she'd be doing if she hadn't come North. She'd be just getting up from her pallet on the floor in her mistress's room and seeing to breakfast. Belle tried not to think about food because her stomach ached with emptiness.

The sudden sound of wagon wheels made Belle quickly seek cover in the thick undergrowth beside the narrow dirt road. Hidden by the weeds she prayed whoever it was would drive on by. Her heart was beating so loudly she just knew the sound of it could be heard back home.

"Hey, you, boy. Come on out."

The male voice froze her. She'd been seen. What should she do? Maybe if she didn't show herself the man on the wagon would think he'd only imagined seeing someone and move on.

"We know you're in there," called another voice—female this time. "We won't hurt you."

To Belle's ears, the girl sounded young.

"I'll bet you're hungry," the male voice added. "We can get you something to eat."

Belle found that offer so tempting she almost stood right then and there, but held off. Suppose they were slave catchers, she asked herself. Although she didn't remember hearing of any catchers who rode with young women, this was the North and maybe such things occurred here.

"It's going to get colder and colder today," the man pointed out. "Wouldn't you rather be someplace warm?"

Belle wanted that, too. Her nights of sleeping on the ground had taken their toll. Her clothes were filthy, her body, as well. She was tired, sore and sick to death of being lost alone in this strange land. For a few moments more she pondered his offers, then decided she didn't care if they were catchers or not; she just wanted to stop running.

Bolstered by the last of her courage, Belle stood to meet her fate. To her surprise, the young man and girl had brown skin just like hers. They were Colored, she saw with astonished eyes, and were more finely dressed than anyone she knew back home. The man had on a well-tailored brown suit, his female companion a simple gray cloak and matching bonnet that fit her as if it had never belonged to someone else.

He was walking in the brush toward her and even as Belle took a wary few steps backward, she realized he couldn't be but a few years older than she. He was handsome, too. The dark brown skin and matching eyes made up a face that had very pleasant features. "I won't hurt you," he assured her in a gentle voice. "What's your name?"

"Belle."

His brown eyes assessed her dirty face beneath her battered hat, and then her filthy, ill-fitting clothes. "That's a funny name for a boy."

She almost took offense, but being tall and thin, and dressed like a boy, she said instead, "Yes, it is, but I'm a girl."

He had the decency to look chagrined. "Sorry, miss." He then asked, "Are you seeking deliverance?"

Belle paused. It was one of the secret questions. Even though Belle knew how to respond she hesitated because the guide also warned them to be extremely cautious when approached by strangers; some folks, both Black and White, preyed upon runaways for monetary gain.

But with nothing left to lose, Belle replied, "Yes. Is deliverance near?"

He assessed her for a long moment more before offering, "Yes, it is."

Belle wanted to drop to her knees and weep with joyful relief. She knew he could see the sheen of tears in her eyes, but he left her her dignity by not calling attention to them.

"My name is Daniel Best and that's my sister, Josephine, back there on the wagon."

Belle looked out at the girl who seemed to be carefully scanning the road ahead and behind, then heard her call out, "Come on, Dani. Bring him along before we're seen."

"He's a *she,* Jo," her brother called back.

Josephine responded with a contrite, "Sorry, miss."

Daniel then told Belle, "My sister's right. This is a well-used road and we need to get you to safety."

"Where?"

"Our house for now. My parents will know what to do. Come on," he said kindly.

Discreetly wiping at the tears on her face, Belle followed him back to the wagon where his sister offered up a winning smile. "Hello, I'm Josephine. Most people call me Jojo." Jojo was small and dark skinned. Long black sausage curls dangled from beneath the edges of her gray bonnet.

"Hello, Jojo. I'm Belle."

"Hello, Belle. How old are you?"

"Sixteen."

"Well, I'm twelve, and Daniel's eighteen. He thinks he's a man."

"Quiet down, pest, and move over so she can get in."

Belle watched with amazement when Daniel pushed aside a few large bales of hay and opened a trapdoor in the bed of the wagon.

"It has a false bottom," he explained. "It's not very big or comfortable, but you can hide in here until we get safely home."

Belle looked at the space. It did look rather small, but she didn't think twice. She removed her hat, placed it on her stomach, and squeezed into the coffinlike space. There was just enough room for a thin person like herself to lie flat as long as she placed her arms tight against her body. She could feel cool air coming into the box. Knowing she'd be able to breathe made her relax.

Daniel asked, "Are you ready?"

Belle, lying flat on her back, looked up at him and nodded. "Yes."

"Then I'm going to close the door and put the bales back on top. We'll be home in under an hour."

"Thank you," Belle whispered genuinely.

"You're welcome."

With that said, the lid closed, plunging Belle into darkness.

It was a bumpy, jostling ride. After only a few minutes, Belle wanted to turn over and make herself more comfortable, but it was impossible; she was for all intents and purposes stuck like a too-fat duck in a too-small roaster. To take her mind off of her discomfort, she forced herself to think of other things. Where was her father? she wondered. Did he manage to escape, too, or had he and the others been caught by the slave catchers? Was he out wandering the countryside searching for her? She was terribly worried about him. He'd face dire consequences if he had been caught and sent back South because he'd run before. He could be sold, beaten or even killed for attempting to give her a better life. Her biggest fear was that she'd never see him again. Belle didn't want to cry because she couldn't raise her arms to wipe away her tears, but there in the dark, the tears came anyway.

The wagon came to a halt a while later. Still hidden, Belle hoped they were at their destination because the narrow space seemed to be shrinking and pressing in on her from every side. To her relief, she heard footfalls on the bed above, and then Daniel's voice.

"We'll have you out in just a minute, miss."

True to his word the door opened and Belle's eyes closed with relief. Daniel offered a hand out. Belle twisted herself until she could raise her arms, then grabbed hold. His grip was strong and sure; his skin warm against her own. Moments later, she was free, and he helped her down from the wagon as if she were a princess instead of a runaway he'd found hiding in the brush.

"Come on, Belle," Jojo called. "You have to meet Mama. Papa's away at a convention."

Belle forced her attention away from the handsome Daniel, now undoing the tack from the horses, then followed Jojo into the house.

They entered by way of the kitchen. A wary Belle looked around at the small, homey space with its cupboards, sink and sideboard of china, and found the interior no different from kitchens back home. How would Jojo's parents receive her, though? Would they really take her in?

Jojo said, "Come on, Belle. Mama's going to be so pleased. We never had a girl here before."

Belle swallowed her trepidation and once again let Jojo lead the way. The kitchen led to a parlor of sorts that had drapes on the windows and a large blue upholstered settee with a beautifully crocheted doily across the back. Having been owned by a seamstress, Belle knew fine needlework when she saw it, and the long, oblong piece definitely fit that definition.

"Mama, this is Belle."

Jojo's voice snapped Belle's attention back. She found herself looking into a pair of kind brown eyes reminiscent of Daniel's. She was a tall, gracefully thin woman, and had a smile that allayed all Belle's fears. Just seeing her made Belle know for certain that yes, she was finally safe. She dashed away more relieved tears, not wanting Jojo's mama to think she was a weak sniveler.

"Welcome to our home, Belle."

Belle nodded, then said politely, "Thank you."

"You're all alone?"

"Now I am, ma'am."

Mrs. Best studied Belle for a moment, then said to her daughter, "Jo, heat some water for our guest. Belle, have a seat."

Belle looked over at the settee and the matching upholstered chairs, and said, "I'll just stand. I'm too dirty."

"Sit, Belle."

Belle held her eyes.

The woman gestured to the settee. "You've probably come a long way and have earned the right to sit wherever you please."

Belle sat on the floor.

Jojo's mama smiled and shook her head. "As you

wish then. Now, tell me how you got to Michigan. Where're you from?"

"Kentucky."

Belle then told her story. She began with the escape from Kentucky over a month ago and ended with the disastrous run-in with the slave catchers.

"And you were separated from your father?"

"Yes, ma'am. Five days ago. Do you think they caught him?"

"I don't know, dear, but our Vigilance Committee will do all it can to answer that question for us. How many catchers were there?"

"Six, eight. I'm not certain. What's a vigilance committee?"

"A group of our people who've dedicated themselves to doing all they can to protect and uplift the race. There are committees in towns all over the North."

Belle had never heard of such a thing. "And they'll help me?"

"Yes, they will," Mrs. Best reassured her kindly. "If your pa got away and was picked up by another conductor, they'll let us know. What about your mother, did she make the trip North?"

Belle shook her head sadly. "No. Mama was sold when I was nine."

Mrs. Best nodded sympathetically. "Well, let's get you a hot bath and something to eat."

Belle nodded behind a yawn. Now that she'd found a haven, she was so sleepy and tired she could hardly move.

Daniel came in then. Belle again thought him the handsomest boy she'd ever met but kept her eyes low lest she be caught staring. He asked his mother, "Will she be staying with us?"

"For now, yes. How's your sister coming with that water?"

He glanced Belle's way for a moment and their eyes held. He then turned back to his mother. "She has it heating."

"Good. Did you get to finish your route?"

"No, we came straight home after finding Belle. I'll finish tomorrow."

Belle suddenly felt guilty. "I'm sorry. I didn't know you had to cancel your errands because of me."

"It's a newspaper route," he explained. "I deliver Mr. Fred Douglass's paper. A day's delay won't hurt anything."

Belle hated to sound ignorant, but asked, "What's a Fred Douglass's paper?"

Daniel explained. "Frederick Douglass is one of our greatest leaders, and he publishes his own newspaper. At first he called it the *North Star* but now it's *Frederick Douglass's Paper*. You've never heard of him." It was a statement not a question.

Belle felt ignorant. "No."

His mother stood. "Belle, you'll have plenty of time to learn all you need to know about the North, and you may even get an opportunity to meet the famous Mr. Douglass before all's said and done, but right now, let's see to your comfort."

Belle followed in Mrs. Best's wake. Unable to stop herself, Belle gave a quick glance over her shoulder at Daniel. He was watching her, too. Embarrassed, she flashed back around. He probably thought her the dirtiest, smelliest girl he'd ever met, she told herself, and focused her attention on following his mother.

She showed Belle into a small bathing room off the kitchen. Belle looked around. There was a hip tub in the center of the plank floor. She assumed the facilities were behind the screen set up near the opposite wall. The fire in the grate was high and hot, making the room warm and toasty.

"We should probably wash your hair first."

Belle agreed. She'd been sleeping on the ground and in barns. Her hair was probably as filthy as the rest of her. Belle ran her hand across the short, rough surface. It was so tangled and matted, trying to comb through it would be useless, so she knelt facing the tub. Leaning her head over the edge, she put her fingers in her ears and waited for Mrs. Best to slowly pour the buckets of water over her hair.

"It might be a bit hot," Mrs. Best cautioned.

It was, but not too hot. It took two buckets to get the hair wet enough to lather up with the soap. Soon, however, Belle's hair was filled with suds. Three rinses later it was soft, wooly and clean. She wrapped her head in a clean towel and sighed, satisfied.

Mrs. Best looked pleased. "I'll give you some oil for your hair after your bath. Are you ready to have the tub filled again?"

Belle used the edges of the towel around her head to catch the rivulets of water running down her cheeks and into her ears. "Yes, ma'am."

Mrs. Best took the hip tub outside and emptied it. After it was filled again from the cauldrons on the stove, Belle was left alone to undress. Taking off her boots and socks showed why her feet were so aflame. Just as she'd guessed, her soles had been rubbed raw and were covered with stinging blisters. Belle didn't plan on saying anything to Josephine or her mother about her feet, though; the family had been gracious enough to take her in. She didn't want to burden them further with her complaints.

Stepping into the hot water made her feet hurt so much

tears welled in her eyes. She forced herself to stand though, hoping the heat would soothe the pain. The tub was the standard hip tub, only big enough to stand or stoop in. When she could bear to open her eyes again, Belle spent a long time scrubbing herself as clean as she could. Mrs. Best had obviously housed runaways before because she'd had the foresight to leave Belle another hip tub filled with clean hot water. It was as if she'd known the bathwater would be too filthy to rinse with. And it was. Averting her eyes from the grimy sight, Belle got out and hobbled as best she could over to the other tub. Once inside of it, she rinsed, stepped out again and wrapped herself in the towel. Drying herself took only a few moments.

Jojo had left a nightgown and a robe. Belle slipped them on. The flannel felt so soft and gentle against her skin, she hugged herself contentedly. Jojo had also left her a pair of fat wool socks for her feet. Belle slowly made her way over to an old cane chair and gently pulled them on. She hoped the soft wool would cushion the raw spots and blisters well enough so she could walk, but when she stood up and put all of her weight on them, the bright agony made her cry out.

There was a knock on the door.

Jojo. "Belle, are you all right?"

When Belle didn't respond, Jojo took it upon herself to enter. Upon seeing Belle bent over in the chair with her legs stretched out, Jojo's young eyes filled with alarm. "Belle?"

"I'm okay," Belle said, plastering a smile on her now clean face.

Jojo didn't buy it. Keeping one eye on Belle, Jojo called out anxiously, "Mama, something's wrong with Belle."

Mrs. Best appeared in the doorway. "Belle?"

"I didn't mean to cry out, but my feet—"

Mrs. Best hastened in. "Let me see."

"I'm okay."

"Then let me see," she echoed.

Belle knew she was no match for Jojo's mama, so she slowly drew off the socks.

"My Lord!" the woman whispered emotionally. She looked up at Belle. "Why didn't you say something? They must hurt like perdition."

"They do," Belle allowed, "but you've been so nice, I didn't want—"

"Young lady, don't ever hide this sort of thing from me again."

Belle dropped her eyes.

All business now, Mrs. Best told her daughter, "Get your brother."

Jojo left quickly and Mrs. Best knelt to look at Belle's feet again. "You poor lamb, these'll take time to heal. It's a wonder you made it as far as you did."

Daniel appeared. He looked concerned. "You wanted me?"

"Yes, I want you to carry Belle up to your grand-mother's room and then go get Bea Meldrum. Belle's feet look like raw meat."

Belle was mortified at the idea of being carried by Daniel. She'd never had a man carry her anywhere in her whole life. "Mrs. Best, if you'd just show me where the room is, I can walk—"

"No, you can't," she contradicted. "Come on, Daniel."

His eyes caught Belle's for a fraction of a second, then he strode forward. He hefted her up in his arms as if she weighed nothing. She hesitated before putting her hands around his neck, but knowing it was necessary in order to hold on, she did.

Daniel was very conscious of the soft feel of her hands around his neck. Even though Belle was tall for a girl she didn't weigh much; carrying her was easy. He could smell how clean she was and feel the warmth of her body against his chest. He didn't look at her as he carried her through the front rooms and up the stairs to his grandmother's old room. She was a lot prettier than he ever could've imagined beneath all that dirt, and he didn't want to frighten her by staring; she was already shaking like a leaf.

"Put her there on the bed," his mother instructed.

Daniel complied. He avoided looking into Belle's dark eyes. "I—I'll go and get Mrs. Meldrum."

"Thank you. If she's not at home, leave her a note telling her we need her assistance."

"Yes, ma'am."

He forced himself to walk out of the room without looking back at the runaway named Belle.

After Daniel's exit, Mrs. Best explained, "This was my mother-in-law's room, but she died last year. While you're here, it can be yours."

Belle had never had a bedroom of her own. She'd always slept on a pallet on the floor in her mistress's room. "Mrs. Best, I don't need all this space—"

"Get under the covers. Jo, go downstairs and fetch her a bowl of that stew."

Jo left.

"Now, you, under the covers."

Belle surveyed Mrs. Best silently. She saw the determination in the woman's eyes and decided to do as she was told. They could discuss this some other time. Belle got into the bed and was immediately overwhelmed by the luxury of clean, crisp sheets, soft, warm blankets and a mattress that wasn't the cold, damp ground. After the small, bracing bowl of beef stew Jojo brought up, she felt even better.

Fed, she sighed contentedly, then handed the empty bowl to Jojo.

"You look real happy, Belle."

Belle smiled tiredly. "I am, thanks to you and your family."

"Get some sleep," Mrs. Best said. "We'll send Daniel out later to see about a set of free papers for you. For the time being you'll be my niece."

Belle thought she heard something about free papers and nieces but couldn't be sure. She was already asleep.

two

Belle slowly came awake. When her eyes first opened she had no idea where she was or how she'd come to be in this bed. Then, as she saw the smiling Jojo seated in a chair by the window reading, she smiled in reply. "So, I didn't dream you?"

"No. You're here and you're safe. It must've been awful having to run from the catchers like that."

Belle thought back on that nightmare encounter in the trees. "It was." The mounted catchers and their blood-hounds had descended on the small group of runaways like specters from hell. She shivered, remembering the people screaming, the dogs barking and the guns. She could still hear her father's anguish-filled voice imploring her to run, and relived the terror that grabbed her once she realized they'd become separated and that she was alone. What had become of him?

Jojo's soft voice brought her back. "I'm sorry, Belle. I'm supposed to be here making sure you're okay, not making you sad."

Belle shook off the memories. "It's all right, Jojo. What day is it?"

"Wednesday. You've been asleep two whole days."

Belle stared. "Two days?!" She flung back the covers and made a move to get up. "Your mother must think I'm the queen of the lazybones. My goodness, Jojo, why didn't somebody wake me?"

But as soon as Belle saw the thick bandages swaddling her feet, she froze.

Jojo chuckled at the stunned look on Belle's face. "Guess you will have to stay in bed, Miss Queen of the Lazybones. Mrs. Meldrum came by after you went to sleep and fixed your feet. You're not to walk on them until she says you can."

"And how long will that be?"

Jojo shrugged. "I think she told Mama a week."

"A week?"

"Yep. Mrs. Meldrum said resting will help you get your strength back, too."

Belle had no idea what Mrs. Meldrum had done to her feet, but they weren't paining her as much and for that she was very grateful. She didn't like the idea of being in bed for a week though; she'd never been sick a day in her life. "Jojo, I can't be in bed for a week."

"Why not?"

Belle had to think about it. "Well—"

"Do you have any engagements or appointments?"

"No, but—"

"So you can be in bed for a week."

"No, I can't. I'll get delirious in here with nothing to do."

"Do you want something to read? Daniel's room has more books than the lending library."

"No." Belle couldn't read, a fact she wished to keep to herself for now. "Is there any sewing that needs to be done?"

Jojo's brown eyes lit up. "Is there? I have a banner to

finish for my church group and I've made a mess of it. Can you sew?"

"Yes."

"Do you think you can untangle the threads for me?"

"I can try," Belle responded encouragingly.

Jojo quickly left the room. Moments later she returned carrying a folded length of indigo satin. She laid it out across Belle's lap. There were some embroidered words that meant nothing to the illiterate Belle, but she understood stitches and these weren't done very well at all. The threads in some of the words and in the embroidered United States flag were uneven, twisted and misshapen. "What's going in these spaces?" Belle asked, indicating two chalked-in squares.

"The Liberian flag and the flag of Haiti. I was hoping that if I put off doing them long enough it'd be too late to enter the competition and I wouldn't have to finish it."

Belle eyed the banner critically while asking, "This is for a contest?"

"Yes, all the young women at church are competing. The best banner will be presented to Mr. Douglass when he comes to visit this summer."

As Belle fingered some of the stitches, Jo added dejectedly, "This one won't win a prize, will it?"

Belle didn't lie. "No."

Jo sighed frustratedly. "I told Mama I don't have the talent, but she insisted I enter. She says all young women should be accomplished seamstresses."

"She's right."

Jojo looked disheartened.

"We can fix this though."

Jojo brightened. "Are you certain?"

"Positive. Go and get your threads and scissors."

* * *

So for the next hour, Belle did her best to remove some of the fouler stitches, while Jojo looked on.

Belle asked, "Tell me why you picked these two flags."

"Well, both mean something special to the race. Thanks to the great General Toussaint-Louverture, the Haitian slaves freed themselves from the French and in 1804 Haiti became a Black nation."

Belle didn't know that. "What about Liberia? Where is it?"

"Western coast of Africa. It became a Black republic back in '47. Folks who wanted to go back to the Mother Continent live there."

Jo then turned her attention back to the banner. "I tried to make the star straight, but I guess I didn't do it real well."

"You did a good job, considering."

"Considering one of Mrs. Meldrum's chickens could've done better."

Belle grinned. "My papa used to say we all have talents, just in different things. What's yours?"

"I'm going to be a hairdresser," Jojo boasted proudly.

"Really?" Belle delicately cut out some of the threads in the embroidered words, then pulled the stitches free.

"Yep, but Mama wants me to go to Oberlin like Daniel—"

"What's Oberlin?"

Jojo looked at her strangely for a moment.

Belle was embarrassed. "I don't know about a lot of things here, Jojo."

Jojo nodded understandingly. "I'm sorry, Belle, I forgot. How about this, whenever you don't know something you just ask me. I won't make fun of you."

In that moment, Belle knew that no matter what the

future held or where it led, Jojo Best had earned a place in her heart. Grateful tears stung her eyes. "I'd like that. So tell me about this Oberlin. What is it?"

"It's a college in Ohio."

Belle couldn't hide her surprise. "There were colleges back home, but we weren't allowed to go, of course. This Oberlin let Daniel go?"

"Sure. Oberlin lets everybody in. Men, women. It's been letting our people study there since 1835."

Belle was impressed. "And they let our folks study right next to the Whites?"

"Yep."

Bell shook her head in wonder. "My papa was right. Things are different up here. Tell me this, how old do you have to be before they let you study there?"

"Old enough to have finished your secondary education and be able to pass the entrance examinations. Most new students are at least fifteen. Dani finished the men's program in just a few months."

"He must be very smart."

"He is. Mama says education is crucial to one's upbringing—that and knowing the history of our people."

"Why?"

"Because we can't tell others about our accomplishments if we don't know them ourselves."

Belle thought that made perfect sense. "Well, Jojo, I want to know as much as you."

Jojo smiled. "You will, don't worry, and with Mama around you'll learn whether you wish to or not."

The girls laughed, then went back to the banner.

After a while, Belle asked, "What does your papa do, Jojo?"

"He's a cabinetmaker. His shop is in the barn behind the house. Dani's his apprentice."

"You said he's at a convention. What happens at a convention?"

"People come from all over, and it's mostly a lot of speeches. They talk about slavery, how to make the government treat us with respect, what folks should be doing to make the race greater. Things of that sort."

"Do all races attend these conventions?"

"Some of them, but usually at ours, it's just us. This one is in Philadelphia, so folks from all over the North will probably be there."

"Women, too?"

"Sometimes. Usually Mama and the other ladies have their own gatherings. A lot of men don't want the women helping with the thinking."

"Why not?"

"Mama says because the women will get things done and not stand around all day puffing and pontificating like the men do sometimes."

Belle chuckled. "Have you ever been to one of these conventions?"

"A few times. I went the time Mama spoke down in Toledo."

Belle paused. "Your mother speaks?"

"Sure. Mama's pretty famous as a speaker. She even went to England a few years ago to meet with some anti-slavery ladies there. She has friends all over the world."

Belle found all this a bit hard to fathom. Where she came from Black women were allowed to speak, too but only when told what to say and when to say it, she mused sarcastically. They most certainly didn't talk about going against slavery or travel to England. Smiling to herself, Belle thought she might like being up North.

They were interrupted a short time later by the entrance of Mrs. Best carrying a bed tray. "Belle, I brought you something to eat. Are you up to it?"

Belle set aside Jojo's banner. "Yes, ma'am."

Jojo spoke up contritely, "Oh, Belle, I'm sorry. I was so excited about you fixing the banner, I didn't even ask if you were hungry."

"It's all right," Belle told her genuinely. "We were having so much fun, I forgot about my stomach, too."

Mrs. Best shook her head, amused. "Some nurse and patient you two are. Luckily, mamas have good ears. I could hear you two laughing, so I knew Belle was awake."

On the tray sat a bowl of maple-sweetened oatmeal and a small dish of spiced apples. Mrs. Best placed the tray down on Belle's lap, saying, "Jo's showing you her banner, I see."

Jojo said, "Mama, Belle's excellent with a needle. She's fixing my stitches."

"Really?" Mrs. Best picked up the indigo banner and looked it over. Her eyes, full of wonder, slid to Belle. "You did this stitching?"

Belle tried to answer around the apples in her mouth. "Yes."

"Were you a house slave?"

"No, ma'am. I was owned by a seamstress. I've been sewing since I was eight."

"And you're sixteen now?"

Belle nodded. The spiced apples were so good.

"Now, don't take offense, but your speech is so crisp and clear—"

"Mrs. Grayson wouldn't let me visit her customers at home until I could speak properly. She said she couldn't have me slurring like a field hand, embarrassing her and her shop, so she gave me elocution lessons each evening before I went to sleep."

Mrs. Best eyed Belle's precise needlework again. "You're very good at this, Belle."

"Thank you." Belle's talents with a needle had been well-known back home and she'd taken great pride in her work. It pleased her knowing many of her gowns were in the closets and trousseaux of some of the wealthiest women in Kentucky, even though she'd never been allowed to fashion one for herself. "Some of the ladies said I was the best needle-woman in Kentucky, slave or White."

Mrs. Best grinned. "That's quite a testament."

Belle nodded. "Yes, it is."

"Well, maybe you'll want to do that for a living once you get settled."

"Do what, ma'am?"

"Be a seamstress, of course."

Belle stared.

"You have the talent. You might even be able to open up your own shop one day."

Having been a slave all her life, Belle had never considered such a possibility. She loved sewing more than anything. The idea of being able to have her own place made her glow inside. "That would be fine, wouldn't it?"

"I think so, yes."

Belle lay back on the pillows and thought about it some more. "That would be fine."

Mrs. Best chuckled. "Well, we have to get you back on your feet first."

Daniel appeared in the doorway. Beside him stood a man Belle didn't know.

"Papa!" Jojo squealed. "You're back!" She ran to him and he caught her up in a strong, smiling hug.

Their loving reunion made Belle's heart sting for her own father. Would she ever feel his strong hug again?

"You been keeping yourself out of trouble?" Mr. Best asked his daughter.

Daniel cracked drolly, "No."

"Yes, I have," his sister tossed back.

Mrs. Best glided smoothly into her husband's arms. "You're home," she whispered in a tone shot through with relief and happiness.

Much to Belle's embarrassment they shared a short kiss. Mr. Best looked like an older version of Daniel. He had the same dark brown face and tall frame. Still holding his wife within the circle of his arms, he asked her, "How are you?"

"Better, now that you're home safe."

He looked over at Belle who was doing her best not to stare. "Is this the visitor Daniel told me about?"

Mrs. Best nodded. "Yes. This is Belle. She's going to stay with us for a while. Belle, my husband. William, this is Belle."

"Pleased to meet you, sir."

"Same here, Belle. Welcome to our home."

"Thank you, sir."

"How far'd you come, Belle?" he asked.

"Kentucky, sir."

"That's quite a ways."

"Yes, it is."

"Well, you rest yourself and we'll talk. Daniel says you need to find your father."

"I do."

He nodded. "Me and the committee'll do our best."

Belle had no idea if the committee would be successful, but she prayed they would be.

Mrs. Best, looking up at her husband with love in her eyes, asked him, "Are you hungry?"

"Starved. They didn't serve us on the train."

"Then come with me." She took him by the hand. "Belle, will you be all right?"

"Yes, ma'am."

"I'll stay with her, Mama," Jojo offered. "That is, if Belle doesn't mind my company."

"I don't."

And in truth she didn't. Belle'd never had the close companionship of a young woman of color before and she enjoyed Jojo's sunny nature. Having Josephine Best at her side might make the transition from slave to free less bewildering. Belle turned her attention to Daniel standing in the doorway talking with his parents. Even though she'd known him for only a few days, and he probably thought about his shoes more often than he did her, her heart beat faster every time he appeared. It was beating that way now and Belle did her best to ignore it; Daniel Best had studied at Oberlin, a place she'd never even known existed until today. What could he possibly have in common with her, an illiterate runaway?

After Mr. and Mrs. Best left to see about a meal, Daniel told his sister in parting, "Be ready at two. I'm not waiting around for you to fix your hair like last week."

Josephine's chin rose. "If I was Franny, you'd wait forty days and forty nights."

"You're not Franny, pest. So be ready."

Jojo mimicked him soundlessly, then stuck out her tongue.

He shot her a warning glance, then politely nodded Belle's way before leaving the two young women alone.

Belle asked, "What was that all about?"

"Piano lessons. He has to drive me over. Last week I couldn't get my hair the way I wanted and he got mad because I made him late for an appointment with Francine the Queen."

Bell couldn't help being amused by Jojo's sneering tone. "Who's Francine the Queen?"

"His supposed fiancée."

Belle went still. So he had a sweetheart. "Why supposed?"

"He hasn't asked her yet, but it hasn't stopped her from acting like the dirty deed's already been done—"

"Jojo!" Belle snorted, laughing. "Dirty deed?"

"I hate her. She's so spoiled and mean. Treats me like a boil."

Belle tried to be diplomatic. "But she has to have some fine qualities, otherwise your brother wouldn't be with her."

"Oh, she's pretty, and got bosoms, but that's about all. Mama doesn't like her much either. Just tolerates her for Dani's sake."

Belle shook her head in gentle amazement. She wasn't sure she wanted to meet this Francine the Queen, but then again, she did, if only to see the type of girl Daniel wanted to marry. With a name like Francine the Queen, Belle doubted she'd be an illiterate runaway. Sighing softly, she finished her oatmeal and apples.

three

In the days that followed, Belle's strength rebounded and her feet slowly healed. One evening, as Belle ate her dinner from a tray in her room, Mr. and Mrs. Best came in to report on the committee's search for her father.

Mr. Best began by saying, "Wish I had more to tell you, Belle, but so far, all we know is that some of the catchers were Otis Watson's men."

Belle hadn't heard that name before. "Who's he?"

Mrs. Best said disgustedly, "A spawn of the devil."

"Owns a livery a few miles away," her husband added. "Made himself rich by catching fugitives."

"Do you think he knows where my father is?"

"More than likely, but we can't just go up and ask him. We're watching him, though."

Belle didn't know if this was supposed to be good news or not.

"Don't worry," Mrs. Best said, "William and the committee have contacted conductors all the way down the line. They move passengers from Chicago to Philadelphia, and from Kentucky to Canada; somebody's bound to hear something soon."

"The sheriff's helping out, too, Belle," Mr. Best added, "so don't give up."

Belle held on to her hope.

On the twelfth day of Belle's stay, Bea Meldrum, the area's healing woman, pronounced Belle's feet recovered enough to wear shoes again. Belle sat on the bed watching the gray-haired, heavyset Bea slowly survey her feet. As Bea gently touched Belle's soles here and there Belle tried not to giggle, but failed.

Bea glanced up, grinning. "Ticklish, are you?"

"Very," Belle replied.

The spectating Mrs. Best and Jojo both smiled.

"Well, if they're ticklish it means they've healed up nicely. Keep putting the salve on them for another few days, and don't tire them or yourself out. Anybody that can teach Jojo here how to make a decent stitch is very valuable to this community."

Jojo's fist went to her hip in mock offense. "Hey, that's not nice," she warned Bea.

All the women laughed in response, then Bea left with a wave.

Jojo asked, "So, what do you wish to do first, Belle?"

"Start earning my keep, if I may, Mrs. Best."

"In what way, dear?"

"I can do chores. I'm a fairly decent cook. Laundry. Whatever help you need."

"How about you just rest up for now. You've had a hard time these past few weeks; the work will still be here when you're ready."

"But—"

"No buts, young lady. In fact, Daniel's going to the train to pick up a package for me. How about I tell him to take you two along? You'd probably enjoy some fresh air."

Belle thought that a splendid idea.

Jojo wasn't so sure. "He's not going to like it, Mama. Says he gets tired of chauffeuring me around."

Her mother ignored that. "Help Belle get dressed." She exited.

So Belle dressed with Josephine's help. Like all of the clothing Belle wore, the faded blue gown and scuffed shoes came from a stash of donated articles Mrs. Best kept for runaways. Because of Belle's height, the hem ended a few inches above her ankles. Belle didn't mind. The garment was far better than anything she'd owned before and she didn't wish to remain cooped up inside the house another minute.

Daniel drove the wagon around to the front of the house, and if he didn't want to play chauffeur he kept it hidden. He had on a nice brown top hat and a matching coat.

Belle knew her attire wasn't nearly as fine. Her hand-me-down cloak and bonnet, though clean, were neither fashionable nor new.

Jojo, ever in charge said, "Belle, why don't you sit in the middle?"

Belle looked up at Daniel, seated behind the reins. Her heart began to pound. "I can sit on the outside."

Daniel told them both, "Come on, you two, I don't have all day."

So Belle picked up her skirts and climbed aboard. Once Jojo took the end spot on the seat, Daniel slapped down the reins and they were under way.

Belle wondered if Daniel could sense her nervousness. Not wanting to draw attention to herself, she sat quietly while Daniel drove and Jojo talked. According to Jojo, the train station was just a few miles away in a town called Ann Arbor.

Jojo couldn't resist the opportunity to needle her brother. "I told Mama you wouldn't like us tagging along, but she said she didn't care how you felt."

He looked her way and retorted, "I didn't know pests could talk."

A grinning Josephine stuck out her tongue. Belle inwardly chuckled. It was quite apparent the siblings cared for each other, and their mock squabblings were just that. Belle soon put them out of her mind, though, because she was so happy to be out-of-doors. The April air still held a trace of the departing winter's chill, but the sun felt warm on her face, and the promise of spring could be seen in the fat brown buds on the trees.

Daniel directed his next words to Belle. "Did Mama show you the papers?"

She nodded. "Yes."

The papers he was referring to were her free papers. The documents verified a former slave's freedom. They also noted the person's description, age and where they were born. Being a runaway, Belle was not legally entitled to have them, but the Bests had secured her a set somehow. "How'd she get them?"

"Papa forged them."

Belle's eyes widened.

He chuckled at her alarmed face. "The slave catchers don't play fair, so why should we? Papa copies real papers, then adds whatever name is needed to the forgeries."

"Is that common?" Belle asked.

He nodded. "All over the North. Papa's even copied my papers a few times for fugitives going through our station."

"But what do you mean by the slave catchers don't play fair?"

"Slave catchers have the right to hunt down runaways because of the Fugitive Slave Act of 1850. We call it the Kidnap Law because there's nothing in it that prevents them from taking anyone they choose, slave or free, and that's what they've been doing. There's been lots of free people taken South just so the catchers can collect a bounty."

"Is that part of the law, too?"

"No. Before a person can be sent back to slavery there's supposed to be a hearing before a magistrate, but many times the catchers jump that step and take them South anyway."

Jojo added bitterly, "And even if there's a hearing, the magistrates are paid more to process the case when the fugitive is sent back."

Belle didn't like the sound of that. "So if I don't have the papers I can be sent back? What if they're lost or get burned up in a fire?"

"Don't worry," Daniel told her. "Mama hid them in a safe place, and Papa filed a duplicate set with the local sheriff. He's a friend, too. And if you ever have to go to court, your papers will stand up. Papa does papers for folks all over this area, and he's never had his work questioned."

Back home, Belle had heard of slaves forging passes so they could escape or travel to visit family and friends, but she'd never personally known anyone bold enough or literate enough to have done it. Even though both Mr. and Mrs. Best offered assurances that the papers wouldn't be challenged either, Belle couldn't help but wonder if the forged documents would survive serious scrutiny. She hadn't expected to be involved in intrigue while seeking freedom. She had naively believed that once she came North her worries would be over.

"Are you warm enough?" Daniel asked her.

Wrapped in the heavy cloak, Belle nodded shyly. Her sixteen-year-old heart warmed at his concern. "Have your parents been helping runaways a long time?"

"Since before Jojo and I were born."

Jojo added proudly, "Mama freed herself by running away from Virginia when she was twelve. Papa was born free in Canada."

"Your mother was a runaway?"

"Yes."

Belle found that information surprising. It had never occurred to her that Mrs. Best was slavery born, but the knowledge gave Belle hope that one day she, too could become as polished and confident as Mrs. Best. Right now, she didn't feel polished at all, but she was a free young woman. That felt good, even if her worries about her father hadn't diminished.

A bit farther down the road they saw a wagon approaching. Jojo said to her brother, "That looks like Trudy's papa's wagon."

"Sure does," he agreed.

Belle asked, "Who's Trudy, Jo?"

"My best friend in all the world. She's been gone two weeks visiting an aunt in Toledo. Drive faster, Dani. I need to see if she's with him."

"I'm not risking the team just for that. You'll have to wait until we get closer."

Jojo was practically falling out of the wagon as she stood, trying to get a better look. "Oh, it is her! Look!"

Jojo started waving for all she was worth. On the approaching wagon stood a dark-skinned girl waving back with the same excitement.

"Stop, Dani! Stop!" Jojo cried.

Smiling and shaking his head, her brother complied. A second later, Jojo jumped down from the wagon and ran pell-mell up the road, cloak flying. Trudy did the same, running to meet her.

Belle had no idea how it felt to have such a loved friend, but seeing them warmed her inside. "They must've really missed each other."

A nodding Daniel watched his sister and her friend hug each other in a laughing reunion, then cracked, "They're both pests."

Belle laughed.

Turning, he held her twinkling black eyes for a moment, then said, "We're never going to get to the station at this rate."

Belle found she couldn't hold his gaze very long.

He asked then, "You always been this shy?"

Belle forced up her eyes. "I guess."

"It's okay to be shy."

She dropped her head again. Being with him made her so tongue-tied she couldn't respond.

Just then, Jojo came running back to the wagon. "Belle, I want you to meet someone. This is Trudy Carr. Trudy, my cousin, Belle. She's staying with us."

Trudy was finely dressed in a sweeping green cloak and a matching velvet bonnet. Her dark eyes held a smile. "Pleased to meet you, Belle. Hello, Dani."

It was easy to see that Belle wasn't the only girl sweet on Daniel.

"Welcome home, pest number two. How was the trip?"

"Fine," she replied as she smiled up at him with cow eyes. "I'm glad I'm home, though."

Jojo rolled her own eyes at her friend's obvious antics, saying, "Dani, do you think Mama would mind if I went home with Trudy? Her papa says he'll bring me home later."

The two wagons were now side by side so Daniel looked over at Trudy's papa and asked, "Are you sure you don't mind, Mr. Carr?"

He cracked, "Gonna have to put up with all that giggling sooner or later. May as well be sooner."

Trudy's fist went to her hip in mock outrage. "Papa!"

He just smiled.

Grinning, Daniel said, "Then they're all yours. I'll let my folks know you'll be seeing her home."

Jojo beamed. "Thanks, Dani."

Daniel then added, "Oh, Mr. Carr. This is our cousin, Belle."

"Pleased to meet you, Belle."

"Pleased to meet you, too, sir."

Jojo climbed onto the Carr's wagon. "Bye, Belle."

"Bye, Jojo. I'll see you later. You and Trudy have fun."

"Enjoy yourself, pests," Daniel said.

The girls answered in unison, "We will."

With a wave, Jojo and the Carrs were off.

In the silence that followed, Daniel said, "Well."

Belle felt shyer and more unsure than ever. "Well."

"Guess we should get going."

Belle nodded.

He then asked, "You sure you're warm enough? I know it's warmer where you're from."

Belle nodded, again too overcome by being alone with

him to form words. *He probably thinks you're a simpleton,* she scolded herself. "How far is the station?"

"Another few miles."

Back home, because there'd been no call for Belle to travel, or to be anywhere but sewing for Mrs. Grayson, she'd never seen a train except in pictures. "I've never seen a train station," she said without thought, then immediately wanted to take the words back.

A simpleton and *ignorant!*

Daniel sensed her discomfort, so he said gently, "That's nothing to be ashamed of. Lots of things will be new here. Think of yourself as a traveler in a strange land, and whenever you need help or have a question, remember we're all here."

Belle hadn't thought about being up North in those terms, but realized Daniel was correct; she was a traveler in a strange land.

"So will you let me know if you need anything?"

Belle looked him straight in the face. "I will."

"Promise?"

Holding his eyes, she said, "I promise."

"Good, now let's take you to see the station."

Belle wondered if she'd ever breathe again.

When Daniel stopped to park the wagon near the depot, Belle's limited knowledge of train stations made it impossible for her to judge whether this station was big or small. There were certainly many people milling about, though: folks of all races. Some were hauling trunks; other stood near the tracks waiting, she assumed, to either board the train or meet someone scheduled to arrive. There was so much to see: buildings, people, faces.

Belle had no idea she was standing up in the wagon until she turned to find Daniel watching her. Embarrassed, she said, "I must be staring like a field hand in the big house. I'm sorry."

"Nothing to apologize for. You're a traveler, remember."

Belle knew he probably extended this kindness to all the runaways he encountered, but it warmed her heart anyway.

Suddenly the air exploded with the loudest sound she'd ever heard in her life. Covering her ears, she stared transfixed at the sight of the big black train barreling down the track, with cinders, sparks and embers pouring from its stack. It looked almost alive! The sight filled her with such exhilaration, she forgot about being sixteen and grinned like she was six. Turning to Daniel she saw him grinning, too.

He asked, "Like it?"

The train slowed, then stopped father down the track. "I never knew they were so big or so noisy. My Lord."

Daniel laughed.

"Is this station a big one?"

People were now stepping down from the train onto the platform.

"No, it's very small. The one in Philadelphia has more tracks than you can count."

Belle found that amazing.

"Do you want to see it up close?"

Belle nodded excitedly.

So with Daniel Best by her side, Belle Palmer got her first real look at a steam engine. It proved to be even noisier up close: noisy, smoky and quite dangerous, too, she realized watching a man snatch his wife's hat from her head and slap at the embers threatening to burn a hole in it.

"The stacks always rain down ashes. Never stand real

close," Daniel advised her as they picked their way through the crowd. He added, "One time in Boston, I left the train station with three burn holes in my spanking-new suit."

Belle met his smile and doubted she'd forget the advice.

Although the engine was made of metal, the four cars it pulled were made of wood. The freight car they were seeking was the last in line.

The light-skinned porter unloading the car greeted their approach with a smile. "Can I help you?" he asked.

"I'm expecting a package," Daniel replied politely.

The porter walked over to the stacked crates and other wrapped items piled nearby. "What's the name?"

"Best," Daniel replied. "Mrs. Cecilia Best."

Belle hadn't known Mrs. Best's given name before now.

It took the porter only a moment or two to find Mrs. Best's leather-bound package. As he handed it over, he glanced at the writing on it. "Says here it came all the way from England."

Daniel took the fat parcel. "My mother has friends there. Thank you, sir."

"You're welcome, son."

As she and Daniel walked back to the wagon, Belle wondered if one day she'd get packages from England, or be able to tell folks about the train station in Philadelphia. Daniel had mentioned being in Boston as casually as she would've mentioned the weather back home. Being free and facing an unknown future was both exciting and scary. Parts of her missed home like the dickens, but other parts wanted to be right here; she kind of liked this thing her papa called freedom. Thinking about him put a damper on her feelings, but she was determined to make him proud. She vowed to learn as much as she could, then become as prosperous as she could so when they were reunited he'd know the sacrifices he'd made on her behalf hadn't been in vain. To that end, she vowed to learn something new every day. Today she'd learned many things, not the least being never stand too close to a train—if the smoke doesn't get you, the brimstone will.

They'd almost reached their wagon when a small group of people standing nearby drew their attention. The group was circled around some activity neither Belle nor Daniel could see.

Belle asked, "What do you think is happening over there?"

Daniel appeared concerned. "I'm not certain, but I recognize some of the people. Come on."

Belle followed.

As they neared, Belle saw anger on the faces of the folks gathered, an anger seemingly directed at the tall, muscular Black man standing stonily in their midst. He seemed to be waiting to board the train, but there were bruises on his face and his clothing was torn and dirty. One of his eyes was swollen shut. Even though it appeared as if he'd been on the losing end of a fight, his chin was raised defiantly. A White man wearing a badge stood at his side and had one hand firmly clamped on the Black man's arm.

Belle was about to ask Daniel what this all meant when a big clod of dirt sailed out of the crowd and hit the Black man full in the face. Another was thrown. Then another. He ducked, but the rocks kept coming, much to the glee of the cheering, jeering crowd. When a rock struck the lawman, he raised his gun. Folks quieted.

The lawman declared, "Next rock thrower's gonna spend the night in jail."

The crowd grumbled.

Someone shouted, "Turn him over to us!"

"Yes!" another voice yelled out. "We'll show him justice."

The murmur in the crowd began to grow. Belle could feel the tension in the air.

Daniel grabbed Belle's arm. "Let's get out of here. Could be trouble."

Wanting to stay and get her questions answered, Belle was about to balk, but Daniel steered her firmly back toward the wagon. "Let's go."

Belle had to practically run to keep up with Daniel's long strides. "Daniel, who was that man?"

"Patterson Riley. He's being escorted out of town."

"Why?"

"For his own safety. Riley works with Otis Watson."

"The slave catcher?!" For a moment, Belle was so stunned she froze in her steps. "He's a slave catcher?"

"Yep."

Belle remembered being told that men of all races were known to prey upon runaways, but she hadn't really believed a man of color would do something so despicable.

Still unable to fathom such treachery, Belle climbed into the wagon and Daniel set the team on the course home.

Belle finally asked him, "What will happen to him?"

"If he makes it out of here in one piece, who knows? Become a traitor somewhere else, more than likely."

"What do you mean, if he makes it there in one piece?"

"Folks up North don't cotton to traitors, Belle. You saw how angry those folks were. In Cincinnati a few years back, a man was tarred and feathered for aiding catchers. Others have simply disappeared or been found dead floating in a creek."

"Did someone around here give him all those bruises?"

Daniel nodded tightly. "Heard he turned himself in to the law because he feared for his life."

Belle could understand why. She'd had no idea such things went on here. How could a man of the race do something so cruel as to send someone back to slavery? Had Riley ever watched a loved one sold? It seemed plain he had not. She had though, and for the first time in a long while Belle let her own dark memories of the auction block rise to the surface of her mind.

She was silent for so long, Daniel finally asked, "What are you thinking about?"

"My mother. She was sold away when I was nine."

Their eyes held for a few silent moments, then she turned to gaze out over the greening fields bordering the road. Her voice softened. "She screamed and fought, but they dragged her away anyway. I hear those screams in my dreams some nights. It was the first time I ever saw my father cry."

Daniel didn't know what to say. He'd always had his mother near; he couldn't imagine having her suddenly torn from his life, though he knew it happened regularly to those who were enslaved. "Have you seen her since?"

"No. She was sold Deep South somewhere. My father tried to find out, but…" Her words trailed off. "She was sold to punish him for attempting to escape. The paddy rollers and their dogs caught him five days out. They beat him until he couldn't stand, then brought him back in chains. Mama was put on the block the very next morning. He was made to watch, as was I. My mistress said she hoped I'd learn a lesson from it."

But the only thing Belle learned that awful day was that at nine your heart could break forever.

Daniel had been helping on the Road since he was twelve, but he'd rarely gotten to personally know any of the many people his family had helped. The nature of the

Road was such that fugitives usually came in the middle of the night and were gone by sunrise. Being born into a staunch abolitionist family, Daniel vehemently denounced slavery whenever the issue was raised; he'd attended rallies, given speeches and been moved by the heart-wrenching narratives offered up by recently escaped slaves at the local antislavery meetings. Hearing Belle's story touched him in a deeper place, though. Maybe because he had a personal connection to her, having been the one to find her that day on the road; maybe because his mother had taken her in and made her a family member of sorts; or maybe because she'd been so nice to Jojo. Whatever the reason, listening to the pain in her voice further strengthened his resolve to see slavery abolished in his lifetime and to help her make the transition from slave to free as painless as possible.

Because Daniel had grown so quiet, Belle wondered if she'd spoken out of turn. "If I'm not supposed to talk about those things you should tell me."

"No, Belle. It's okay. Just thinking is all."

"Well, don't tell Jojo. I don't want her frightened into thinking someone's going to sell her mama, too."

"Don't worry. Jojo's tough, but thanks for wanting to spare her feelings."

"I like your sister."

"She likes you, too."

"You've all been very kind to me."

He looked her way and said sincerely, "You make it easy."

Belle felt her heart swell and she dropped her eyes, but his quiet praise buoyed her for the remainder of the ride back to his parents' home.

four

JOJO came home after dinner brimming with tales of her reunion with her best friend, Trudy Carr. Afterward, she and Belle retired to Belle's room to work on the banner.

"When's Mr. Douglass coming again?" Belle asked as she embroidered in the edges of what would be the Haitian flag.

Jojo looked up from the practice sampler Belle had designed to help her master her stitching. "I think it's August or July. You'll have to ask Mama."

"He's pretty famous?"

"Really famous, Belle. He escaped, just like you, and now he lectures all over the world."

"What about?"

"Being a slave and how slavery ought to be abolished."

"Daniel seems to admire him a great deal."

"As far as Dani's concerned, the sun rises and sets with Mr. Douglass. Mama's not so impressed, though."

"What do you mean?"

"Oh, she respects what he's done for the race and says he's the greatest orator our people have ever had, but she says his home life is a mess."

Belle looked puzzled.

Jojo looked around the room as if to make sure they weren't being overheard, then whispered, "Mr. Douglass has a mistress."

Belle's eyes widened. "A mistress?"

"Yes. Her name is Julia Griffiths, and they were on a ship to England together. Papa said it was just a misunderstanding and nobody really knows if Mr. Douglass was sharing his cabin with her, but Mama and her friends say Fred has feet of clay."

Belle wondered which side of the story was true. "So, who does your mama admire?"

Jojo didn't hesitate. "Frances Ellen Watkins."

"Who's she?"

"A great female abolitionist. She lectures, and writes antislavery tracts and poetry. One of her most well-known poems is 'Bury Me in a Free Land.'"

"Is she White?"

"No, silly, she's as dark as us."

Belle was surprised by that. "And she lectures?"

"Sure, thanks to Maria W. Stewart, women of all races can lecture now."

Belle hated to keep asking the same question, but— "Who's she?"

"Why, she's the first American woman to stand up and lecture in a room that had men in it. Before her time, women could lecture only to women. She was a woman of the race, too," Jojo added proudly.

"When was this?"

"1832."

Belle shook her head in amazement. "Jo, how do you know all this?"

"School. Mama. Papa. Dani. Everyone I know knows these things."

"Except me."

Jojo quieted, then turned into a miniature of her mama. "Belle Palmer, don't you dare fault yourself—it's only because you weren't allowed."

Belle couldn't help but smile. With Jojo around there'd be no feeling sorry for herself. "Then how about we make a pact?" Belle asked.

"Sure, what kind?"

"You teach me to know as much as you, and I'll teach you to be the best needle-woman in Michigan."

"You have a deal."

The grinning young women shook hands, sealing the agreement.

Downstairs, Daniel sat with his parents in the den. There'd been an emergency meeting of the Vigilance Committee called for this evening concerning a newly arrived band of slave catchers. William Best was preparing to leave to attend. Daniel usually accompanied his father to the meetings but not tonight. Tonight, William thought it best to have a man at home, just in case trouble erupted while he was away. He also had freight to move later and so wouldn't be returning until morning.

"So where were the catchers last seen?" Cecilia asked.

"This morning down near Monroe. They were riding with that scoundrel Otis Watson."

Daniel knew that local slave catcher Otis Watson was hated from Michigan to Ohio and back, with good cause; he'd cost many a fugitive their freedom, and wasn't above kidnapping to have his way. Although Watson knew that the Bests were conductors, he hadn't been able to amass the evidence necessary to have Daniel's parents arrested.

Aiding runaways was a violation of the 1850 Fugitive Slave Act, and a felony under federal law.

"How many men were there?" Cecilia asked her husband.

"Seven, according to witnesses."

Daniel told his parents, "I saw Deputy Wells with Patterson Riley at the train station. Riley looked pretty beat-up."

William Best cracked bitterly, "Must've been that justice he ran into the other day. Heard he's lucky he's still alive. Imagine, taking bribes to reveal a fugitive's whereabouts."

Daniel replied. "Well, at least he was exposed."

William agreed. "Yes, but how many more people will have to suffer before he really gets his just desserts? Good thing his name and description were in the newspaper though; otherwise, only the Lord knows how much hurt he could've caused. Guess brigands like Riley need to do more reading and less sneaking around."

Daniel agreed. Riley's name, along with the names of a few other snakes in the grass, had been posted in last week's edition of the *Weekly Anglo-African,* one of the newspapers Daniel distributed. The notice warned its readers to be aware of and on the lookout for the men. Exposing men who preyed upon the race was a tradition begun by the race's very first newspaper, *Freedom's Journal,* published in 1827 by Rev. Samuel Cornish and John Russwurm. Daniel felt good knowing that Patterson Riley would no longer be a threat to the community and that the newspapers he distributed had been responsible.

Daniel asked his father, "Do you think Watson and those men are coming this way?" The last thing the Road needed was a new influx of human bloodhounds.

"All signs point to yes."

Daniel could see the worry on his mother's face. He

could also hear the girls laughing unaware upstairs. "Will Belle have to leave?" he asked.

"Probably," his father replied. "It might be safer for her if she moves on."

Daniel didn't like that idea very much. Belle was an interesting, albeit shy, young woman, and after being with her this afternoon, he wanted to know more about her.

Evidently, his mother didn't care much for the idea either. "We can't just send her on, William. She doesn't know anyone else. If we did, I'd worry every day how she was faring."

"I know, lovey. I like Belle, too. How about we send her up to my sister in St. Catharines?" William offered.

"And have Jane crush the spirit out of her like she tried to do with Jo last summer? No."

Daniel wondered if he should leave the room. His Canadian Aunt Jane was, as his mother described, a religious zealot, and if you didn't spend every waking hour on your knees, you were bound for hell. Jojo had been sent to visit her last summer, but was so unhappy living such a joyless life, she'd astounded everyone by hopping a train and coming home. Daniel knew that his father didn't like to have his sister bad-mouthed, so if his parents were going to argue he wished to be elsewhere.

To Daniel's surprise his father admitted, "You're right, Jane has become more and more eccentric. But if we don't send her there—where? There's no place to hide Belle around here. We can't have her holed up in the loft in Mr. Finney's barn until Lord knows when."

Mr. Finney was a White abolitionist who often hid fugitives in his loft until they could safely proceed across the Detroit River and into Queen Victoria's Canada.

"Then I say we continue to hide her in plain sight as we have been," Mrs. Best declared.

She looked to Daniel and then her husband.

Both men nodded agreement.

William had a few words of caution to add, though. "No more trips out-of-doors for Belle until we find out more about the catchers. Okay?"

Cecilia looked contrite. "Oh, okay. I know you told me to keep her indoors, but she'd been cooped up for so long, she needed the air, and she had a good time. Didn't she, Daniel?"

"Yes, she did," Daniel replied. He had, too, but he didn't think that would matter to his father.

He was correct.

William said again, "Indoors, lovey. It's for her own safety."

When Cecilia showed her husband an exaggerated pout, a smiling William turned to Daniel and said, "Son, make sure you marry a woman you can control. Otherwise you'll wind up with someone like your mother."

Cecilia shot him a mock look of warning, then asked, "Weren't you leaving?"

His smile broadened into a grin, "I've treasured every moment of our lives together, my love."

"Flattery will get you nowhere, carpenter. Now go on with you. Tonight's freight is out there waiting and you're in here flirting. Say good night to your son."

William laughed. "Good night, son."

"Godspeed, Papa."

His father nodded Daniel's way, threw Cecilia a bold wink, then left them alone.

Daniel saw his mother go to the window. She worried

every time his father left home to do the Work, so to distract her, he said, "Belle really did enjoy going out today."

His mother turned back. "Did she? Did she like the station?"

"She'd never seen one before," he related, admittedly still a bit surprised, then added, "But I suppose that isn't that unusual, considering."

"No, it isn't. I'd never seen a train either until I left Virginia."

Daniel thought back on Belle's reaction to the man and woman with the burning hat, and the memory made him smile.

"What're you smiling at?" his mother asked quietly.

He met her eyes. "Nothing really. She—Belle—just looked so excited seeing that train. I felt like a little kid again."

"Daniel, you're not that old—" she pointed out.

"I know, Mama, but—"

"But what, son?"

He thought for a moment more. "I like Belle—not in a sweetheart kind of way, but she's nice. Do you know what I mean?"

Mrs. Best smiled a bit secretively. "I do, and even though you don't like her in a sweetheart kind of way, you have to admit she is a pretty thing. Once your father thinks it's safe for her to become a real member of the community, I expect quite a few young men will come courting."

Daniel didn't know why that idea should bother him, but it did.

His mother began listing Belle's good points. "She's not lazy, she can sew like an angel and she's been so sweet to Jojo. If I had another son, he'd have to marry her."

Daniel laughed. "Then it's good I have Franny. Otherwise you'd have me and Belle engaged before Christmas."

His mother nodded her head. "You always were a smart child."

They both laughed.

The sound of girlish laughter drifted from the room upstairs again. "Sounds like they're having fun up there," Daniel said.

"It's good to have laughter in the house again. It's been so solemn and silent since Gran died. Jo's missed her so much. Belle's been good for her."

Daniel looked toward the stairs. "Yes, she has. She told me her mother was sold when she was nine. She witnessed it."

Cecilia Best shook her head sadly. "There's nothing more painful. I know."

Daniel knew from his mother's stories that both her parents had been sold away. She'd been twelve at the time. Determined to find them, she'd run away that very same night. Her search had been a vain one and she had been lost for days. Hungry and exhausted, she finally stumbled across a farmhouse owned by a Quaker couple. They took her in, fed her and put her on the Road north to Boston. At present, even though Black abolitionists and their Quaker associates were at odds over many things, including the Friends' continued commitment to segregation within their churches, his mother refused to hear a bad word against them. She'd declared many times that the Quakers were the best friends that the race ever had, and if you didn't agree, be prepared to defend yourself and your position.

"You know, Daniel, your father and I have never taken a runaway into our home this way before, but from the moment I laid eyes on Belle—I can't explain it, but I felt as if she belonged here."

"Woman's intuition?" he asked her. Daniel looked back up to where the laughter continued to flow. *What are they laughing about?* he wondered. The sounds drew him in an inexplicable way.

She shrugged. "Maybe, but in many ways, she reminds me of myself when I first came North. I was just as scared as I imagine she was before you found her."

His mother's voice then took on a more serious tone. "Your father's right about keeping her close to the house for a while. Who knows what Watson and his slugs are after. I pray it's not her."

Daniel didn't want it to be either. Like his mother said, Belle was good for Jojo and he loved the pest very much.

Cecilia sniffed the air. "Smells like Jo's doing hair. Go up and tell her to put her toys away and get ready for bed. They can continue their giggling in the morning."

Daniel nodded and headed out of the room.

Upstairs, Daniel poked his head around the open door, then knocked upon it. "May I come in?"

Sure enough, Jojo was doing Belle's hair. The smell from the small brazier being used to heat the irons filled the hallway. Both girls turned at his entrance and Daniel stared dumbstruck at the lovely vision that was Belle. Jojo had used a curling iron on Belle's short hair, making it fuller and glossier. She'd also tied a thin, emerald green ribbon around it and the ribbon ends played fashionably over one shoulder.

"How does she look, Dani?"

A highly embarrassed Belle instantly tore the ribbon free and set it aside on the small mirrored vanity table she was sitting at. "Don't put your brother on the spot like that, Jojo. It isn't fair."

No, it wasn't, Daniel thought to himself. He decided his mother was wrong: Belle wasn't pretty—she was beautiful. That thought bothered him, too. Being on the edge of an engagement, he wasn't supposed to be eyeing anyone else. Since he couldn't answer his sister's initial question honestly, he ignored it and replied instead, "Mama says get ready for bed."

Belle could see him reflected in the mirror behind her. She noticed that he wouldn't meet her eyes, so she wondered if he hadn't answered his sister's question because he hadn't wished to hurt her feelings. Belle knew she was no beauty and no amount of fancy hair doing would change that. At least he hadn't called her ugly to her face, she told herself.

Daniel could see that Belle looked a bit hurt and he was caught between reassuring her that she did indeed look very fine and his strong sense of loyalty to his soon-to-be fiancée, Francine. Since he saw no way out of the dilemma, he said hastily, "Good night. I'll see you two in the morning."

Perplexed by her brother's seemingly odd behavior, Jojo asked after his departure, "Wonder what's wrong with him?"

Belle shook her head, silently intimating that she didn't know.

Later that night, Daniel doused the lamp on his desk and went to stand before the window. It was a clear, cloudless night, not a safe night to be moving freight because the moon lit up everything for miles around. He hoped his father and the others didn't run into trouble.

Daniel had gone on his first Road mission at the age of twelve. His mother had been against it, saying he was too young, but his father had insisted.

"He'll have to start sooner or later because we need all the soldiers we can get," Daniel remembered his father saying, and much to Daniel's delight, he'd been allowed to accompany his father on the very next trip. He found it not as exciting as his twelve-year-old self had imagined. It was January, it was cold, and after sitting in the wagon with his father for two hours waiting for the fugitives they were supposed to transport to show themselves, he wanted nothing more than to be home in his warm bed sleeping as soundly as he knew six-year-old Josephine was.

In the dark, Daniel smiled at the memory. That had been six years ago. Since then, he'd grown up, spoken at rallies, finished the men's program at Oberlin and learned that sitting in a cold wagon meant nothing when compared with the danger fugitives faced in the quest for freedom. He'd met fugitives and prominent abolitionists, and this summer would be able to shake hands with the great Mr. Douglass himself.

In those same six years, the country had grown increasingly divided over the issue of slavery. The Supreme Court's 1858 decision in the Dred Scott case had caused an uproar. In deciding that Mr. Dred Scott was still subject to slavery, Justice Taney had also written that members of the race were so inferior in the eyes of the Constitution that "they had no rights which a White man was bound to respect." It was pointed out quite loudly by Black and White newspapers all over the North that not only were the Southern majority justices wrongheaded in their decision, they'd distorted history in order to make their claim. In 1788, when the Constitution was initially adopted, the nation's free Black population had many recognized rights, including those related to the buying and selling of property, and the ability to seek justice in the courts. When the Constitution was ratified, five of the thirteen states in the Union allowed their Black citizens to be active participants in the ratification of the document and to vote on the issue.

Now there were rumors of war. Many in abolitionist circles believed taking up arms to be the only way to end slavery once and for all. Daniel believed it, too; he saw no indications that slave owners were going to free their captives out of Christian kindness. In fact, Northern newspapers had been reporting on the schemes of some Southern slave owners to move their plantations and slaves to the remote jungles of Central and South America in order to escape the U.S. ban prohibiting further importation of human slaves. Such blatant arrogance infuriated abolitionists, Daniel included. John Brown of Osawatomie was reportedly massing an army now, and if that was true, Daniel planned on being among the first men in line.

Granted, his mother would undoubtedly throw a fit over the idea, but Daniel had always had a serious bent, even as a youngster. He'd preferred books to marbles, and found listening to speeches far more exciting than dipping girls' pigtails into inkwells. His parents often teased him about taking life so seriously, saying he'd been born old, but in Daniel's mind these were serious times. Three million souls were enslaved in various states across the nation, and those seeking freedom by escaping North were being hunted down like rabid animals by slave catchers armed with federal warrants. Yes, Daniel viewed life seriously; he was a Black male living in a country whose constitution counted him as three-fifths of a person. He couldn't afford to be any other way.

Musing upon the slave catchers made him think back on Belle. He realized he didn't know that much about her. He did know that she'd made him smile at the train station this afternoon, and touched a chord within him by relating the tragic story of her mother. If his mother had her way, Belle would live here forever and ever, amen, an arrangement he truly didn't mind; Belle was nice and she seemed to be filling the role of the older sister Jojo had always wanted. But Daniel could still recall how soft she'd felt and how clean she'd smelled that day he'd first carried her upstairs, and those memories coupled with his reaction to how lovely she'd looked in front of the mirror this evening had not evoked siblinglike feelings at all. The way she was beginning to make him feel was much more complex, much more personal. He hoped once the newness of having Belle around the house wore off and he became more accustomed to the sparkling light in her dark eyes and the curve of her smile, wanting to know more about her would fade, and he'd view her with no more passion than the cousin she was pretending to be.

In the meantime, he'd concentrate on doing the Work and looking ahead to a future that included Francine as his wife.

Lying in bed, Belle was thinking, too—about many things: her father, the Bests, Daniel. She'd put them all in her prayers before burrowing beneath the covers. Now as the darkness surrounded her, she thought about herself. What next? Where would she go, who would she become? The thought of all she'd have to learn to be a success here in the North just about made her hair spin. Maria W. Stewart, Frances Ellen Watkins, Frederick Douglass. There was so much to learn. At this juncture, she didn't even know all the things she'd need to learn, but she was very thankful for the Bests, and she'd told God just that. Without them she might still be wandering the countryside lost.

In the end she echoed what she'd vowed this afternoon at the station—she'd learn as much as she could as fast as she could. If her father had been recaptured, maybe she could make enough money as a seamstress to buy his freedom, if his master, Benjamin, was willing. She didn't think he would be willing, though; her father was a skilled laborer, very valuable, and Master Benjamin had never been a kind man. But then, Belle never thought she'd ever be anything but a slave, so in her mind, with the help of the good Lord, anything was possible. She would see her father again; she just knew she would.

five

BELLE'S hopes were dashed a few days later when Mrs. Best asked her to come into the parlor early that morning.

Belle took a seat. She could tell by the somber faces of Mr. and Mrs. Best that something was amiss. Before they could say anything, Belle stated, "It's my father, isn't it?"

Cecilia nodded. "Word has it that he was recaptured and is now on his way back South."

The pain in Belle's heart made her eyes close. She and her father had been so close to freedom. Now? Now, he was on his way back. She knew deep inside that no matter his own fate, he'd want her to live out the dream he'd hoped she'd find here.

William Best pledged sincerely, "Belle, we're going to do everything we can to find him and bring him back— everything."

"If he isn't killed first," Belle added softly. "He's run before."

Mrs. Best agreed. "Sadly, that is a serious possibility."

Belle felt numb, as numb as she'd been watching her mother sold. "Is there anything else?"

Mrs. Best shook her head. "No, dear."

"Then, may I be excused?"

"Of course," Mr. Best told her solemnly. "Of course."

Belle held on to her tears until she reached the privacy of her room. There, as the bright April day filled the interior with sunlight, Belle Palmer put her head in her hands and sobbed out her grief.

Later that day, Belle's sad mood was interrupted by a knock on the door. "Come in," she called.

It was Daniel. Belle had been crying all day. She knew she probably looked a fright, but didn't care. "Hello, Daniel."

"Hello, Belle."

Daniel had just returned from putting up flyers about this weekend's antislavery rally. His parents had related the terrible news about Belle's father. Seeing her pain filled him with an overwhelming urge to pull her into his arms and shoulder some of her sorrow. "I know nothing's going to cheer you up, but would you like to take a walk or something?"

Belle wondered if he'd come up here on his own, or if his mother had sent him. Either way, she appreciated the kindness. "Thanks, but I'll be all right."

"Not if you spend your day brooding. Would your father want that?"

Belle shook her head no. Wherever he was, living or dead, he wouldn't want her to worry about him, but how could she not? "He was the most important person in my life, especially after Mama was taken."

"Did the two of you live together?"

"No. He was a bricklayer. He and his master traveled around, but after Mama was sold, he never missed a Sunday. Not in seven years."

Daniel appeared confused by her last words, so she explained further: "Many slaves are allowed to visit their kin on Sundays as long as they have a pass from the master and get back before the horn blows them to work Monday morning. He'd come every Sunday."

Belle paused as the memories rose. "I'd wait on my mistress's porch watching the road. Soon as I'd see him I'd fly down the steps and run to meet him. He'd grab me up and say, 'Hey, June bug, you're prettier every Sunday morning'."

Daniel saw the tears in her eyes and the watery smile.

Belle whispered, "I miss him so much...."

Daniel's heart twisted. "Aw, Belle. Don't cry. Come here...."

The next thing she knew he was holding her against his chest and she was sobbing all over the front of his red plaid shirt.

Daniel didn't know what else to do, so he held her tight, stroked her soft hair, and murmured nonsensically. He kissed the top of her brow and told himself if he'd received such tragic news he'd need comforting, too. He could feel the warmth of her limbs against his and smell the scents in the oil Jojo had given her for her hair. Solace was all he was supposed to be offering, but holding her so close evoked stirrings that had more to do with him as a male and less to do with a show of sympathy.

"Daniel Best! What in the world are you doing?!"

The familiar voice struck Daniel like a bolt of lightning. He swung himself around and stared into the furious tan eyes of Francine, his soon-to-be fiancée. Beside her stood his mother. He wondered why his mother seemed to be smiling.

Francine snapped, "For heaven's sake, turn her loose!"

Daniel hastily separated himself from Belle, who, wiping at her damp eyes, appeared equally as embarrassed. Daniel had been so content holding Belle, he hadn't even realized she was still in his arms when he swung around.

"Now," Francine said with a fake smile on her golden, doll-like face, "an explanation, please."

Mrs. Best took over. "Belle, this is Francine Fleming. Francine, Belle Palmer."

"And she is?" Francine asked shortly, looking Belle up and down critically.

"A guest," Mrs. Best replied with just a touch of bite.

The firm tone in Cecilia Best's voice seemed to get the young woman's attention. Evidently she'd tangled with Daniel's mother and lost before, because Francine suddenly found her manners. "How are you, Belle? Excuse my outburst. Daniel's my intended. I'm sure you must know what a shock it was for me to find you two in such a—delicate situation."

Belle now understood Jojo's aversion to the beautiful Francine the Queen, but returned politely, "I understand. I received some bad news today. Daniel—" Belle looked to him for a moment, then added as she turned back to Francine's cool eyes "—Daniel was comforting me is all. I'm sorry his generosity upset you."

Daniel felt like a child caught with his hand in the cookie jar, and he didn't like the feeling at all. He cared very deeply for Francine, but at times she tried to ride him as if he were already saddled, and this was one of those times. "Belle's father was taken back to slavery, Franny. She's had a rough time of it."

Francine, swathed in a sweeping cape made of fine blue wool, replied, "That's terrible. You have my sympathy, Belle."

Francine then turned to Daniel. "Were you planning on

escorting me to Cissy's tonight or not? She needs to know so she'll have the correct number of place settings."

Daniel's jaw tightened. Belle's world had fallen apart and all Francine could think about was a dinner party. He looked to his mother and saw the ice in her eyes. "Let's talk downstairs," he told Francine.

Francine turned to leave. With a dismissive wave of her hand she said, "Been a pleasure meeting you, Betsy."

Belle's chin tightened as she met Daniel's eyes.

He looked grim. "I'll see you later, Belle."

Belle nodded.

His departure left Belle and Cecilia alone.

Cecilia drawled, "Belle, you'll learn that no one's problems are more pressing than Franny's. I can't wait to see what kind of grandchildren William and I are going to get."

"You don't like her either." It was a statement, not a question.

"No, child, I don't. Every day, I pray I'll wake up and be told she's gone to California to mine for gold."

Belle laughed; she couldn't help herself.

Downstairs, Daniel escorted Francine into his father's small study and closed the door. She flounced down onto one of the chairs like a petulant child, saying, "I do have a reason to be angry, you know."

"No, you don't."

"Daniel Best, you were practically kissing that girl. Whatever is your mother thinking of, keeping a fugitive above stairs, anyway? Shouldn't she be off to Canada or some such place?"

In the past few months, Daniel and Francine seemed to be butting heads more and more often over his commitment to the Cause. Francine had been free all of her life.

Although her wealthy widower father was a member of the Vigilance Committee and donated generously whenever called upon, she herself didn't give a hoot about abolitionism or its ancillary issues because it didn't affect her personally, or so she maintained. She'd much rather Daniel spend his time taking her shopping or attending balls than waste the day away setting the groundwork for political rallies or distributing broadsides. "Belle's a guest."

"She's a fugitive, Daniel."

"So was my mother, and at one time, your parents."

"But neither of us knows anything about that. Slavery is an abomination, yes, but we're all free now."

"There are three million slaves in this country, Francine. Half are women and children."

"Oh, please," she drawled out tiredly. "Must we discuss this now?"

"Yes, we must, because this is part of my life and it's going to be part of *our* life if we marry."

She threw up a gloved hand. "I know, I know. I'm sorry, but I won't have runaways sleeping in my bedrooms, Daniel. We need to get that settled now."

She opened her small reticule and extracted a miniature pot of rouge. Using the mirrored lid to guide her, she touched up the color on her lips, then put the pot back inside. "Are we agreed?"

"No."

She eyed him for a few silent moments, then stated, "You're angry at me, aren't you?"

"Yes, I am."

"Why, because I got upset about you hugging that ill-dressed little runaway?"

Daniel's lips thinned, then he simply shook his head. "No.

It's a lot of things. Mostly it's that you don't seem to care about what's happening in the world around you, Francine."

She chuckled a bit sarcastically. "I know you're upset when you address me as Francine—"

Getting up from the chair she came over to him and placed her arms around his waist. Looking up at his chiseled face, she cooed, "Kiss me so I'll know no matter what, you still love me."

Smiling, she softly pressed herself against him and Daniel closed his eyes in response to the reaction that caused. Eighteen-year-old Francine was a well-brought-up, well-educated young woman from a good family. She was also what some folks called a "fast girl." Since they were fourteen, Franny'd let him kiss her and touch her in ways that would get him a beating if their fathers ever found out. In fact, she was so fast Daniel didn't know what to do with her sometimes, like now.

"Kiss me," she whispered again in a voice as seductive as Eve's.

As if Daniel were Adam being tempted in the Garden, he pulled her closer and complied.

When they finally ended the kiss, Francine held him tight and laid her head on his chest. She instantly felt the moisture left behind by Belle's tears. She stepped back. "Ugh, your shirt's all wet!"

Daniel touched his hand to his shirtfront. Memories of Belle surfaced but he pushed them away. "Sorry."

Francine rolled her eyes impatiently. "So, are we going to Cissy's tonight or not?"

He nodded. Francine was both smart and beautiful; he'd never been able to stay angry with her, no matter how frustrated she made him. Lately, however, it seemed to be taking him longer and longer to get over the frustration and to remember that he loved her. He was also beginning to wonder if he'd made a mistake two years ago when he promised Franny's dying mother that he'd take care of Francine always. "Yes, what time?"

"About half past five."

"With those slave catchers about, we shouldn't be out late tonight."

"I know, and I wish someone would do something about them. It's going to be warm again soon. We can't have them ruining all our evenings."

Daniel smiled and shook his head. "You're something, do you know that?"

"Yes, I am," she tossed back with certainty. "But I'm all yours and you're all mine. Now, kiss me again so I'll know that girl upstairs means nothing to you."

Daniel grinned down. "You've had enough kisses for today and that door there's been closed long enough for my mother to come knocking wondering what we're doing in here."

She pouted prettily. "Your sense of honor can be very tiring sometimes, Daniel Best."

He kissed her forehead. "See you this evening."

"Oh, all right."

Daniel went to the door and opened it. Francine sashayed by him and he escorted her outside to her buggy and the waiting liveried driver.

"Later, darling," Francine cooed.

A blink of an eye later, her fancy rig was moving down the street. Daniel turned to head back inside. He glanced up at the house, and just as he did, he saw the curtains in the window of Belle's room drop. Had Belle been watching him or had it been his mother? he wondered. Unable to answer, he resumed the short trek to the front door.

* * *

Cecilia turned from the window. "Well, she's gone."

Good riddance, Belle thought, but kept the opinion to herself. "How long have she and Daniel known each other?"

"All their lives. Franny decided in primary school that Daniel was the one for her and it's been that way since."

"Sounds like a girl who knows what she wants."

"And what she can't get, her papa will buy for her. She's terribly spoiled."

Belle got that impression. "Is she an abolitionist?"

"Her father is. She's a shopper. We practice Free Produce here, but Franny continues to order her gowns from questionable sources."

"What's Free Produce?"

"It's a movement designed to punish slave owners in their pocketbooks. Free Producers don't purchase any goods made by captive hands."

Belle found that idea quite impressive. "None?"

"None. No American sugar, cotton, leather goods. Nothing. It was a campaign started by the Quakers but our communities have embraced it, too."

"So what did you mean when you said Francine was ordering her gowns from questionable sources?"

"You're a seamstress, Belle. Have you ever seen British cotton?"

"On a few occasions, yes. It's coarser and a bit harder to work with."

"Well, Free Produce women buy the higher-priced British cotton for their gowns because England doesn't have slaves. Those ladies who can't afford the British cotton make do with their old ones."

"Francine doesn't?"

"No. She tells her father she orders from Windsor and

Quebec, but in truth she buys American fabric. Admitted as much to Daniel. Said she didn't like the way it chafed her skin."

"But she's helping slave owners."

Cecilia shrugged. "Doesn't seem to matter to her. That's why I was hoping Daniel would find him someone new while away at Oberlin, but he didn't. My son is a strong, dedicated young man. The issues of the day mean a great deal to him and he deserves a woman as special as he."

"Not Francine."

"Not Francine."

Belle knew she'd never be his choice, but the idea of having Cecilia Best as a mother-in-law seemed grand. "Well, maybe he will find someone."

Cecilia looked Belle in the eye and said, "I'll keep praying."

Cecilia headed to the door, but before exiting, looked back. "If you need anything, and I do mean anything, to get you through this heartbreak with your father, let us know."

Belle nodded. "I will, and thank you—for everything."

"You're very welcome. Dinner at five."

"Yes, ma'am."

Jojo had spent the day at Trudy's. Because there was no public school for the area's children of color, the parents who could afford to do so pooled their funds and paid for the services of private tutors. Jojo and her fellow class-mates had been without a formal instructor since their old one moved west last fall. The new teacher, a young man from Chatham, Ontario, had been hired only days ago. Under the agreement, classes would be taught within the homes of the children on a weekly rotating basis and they began this morning.

"How'd the day go?" Belle asked Jojo, who came up to Belle's room after her arrival home.

Jojo took one look at Belle's red-rimmed, swollen eyes and said quietly, "Mama told me about your papa. You must feel awful."

"I do."

"Did Mama give you one of her hugs? They always seem to help me feel better."

Belle wondered if she'd ever meet anyone with a bigger heart than Josephine Best. "No, but Daniel did."

Jojo smiled. "Good."

"Well, up to a point. Francine saw us."

Jojo's eyes widened. "She was here?!"

"In this very room, and she was furious when she saw your brother holding me."

"See, this is why I don't like going to school. I miss everything."

Belle chuckled. "It wasn't all that much really. But she was pretty angry."

"Was she all gussied up?"

Belle shrugged. "I suppose. She had on a beautiful blue cape. I see why Daniel wants to marry her—she's very beautiful."

Jojo waved a dismissive hand. "On the outside maybe, but inside she's rotten as spoiled eggs."

Belle decided to change the subject. It was plain Jojo had no love for her brother's intended. "Tell me about the school. What's the teacher like?"

Jojo swooned dramatically and fell back onto Belle's bed. "He's heavenly. So very, very heavenly. Trudy and I couldn't take our eyes off him. His name's Mr. Hood. He's tall, even taller than Dani, and his eyes—oh, Belle—they're a handsome brown, and he's fit, not fat like the teacher we had last time. I think I could study with him twenty-seven hours a day, ten days a week."

Belle enjoyed Jojo so much. "That handsome, huh?"

"Handsomer. And his voice," she gushed. "He was reading the geography lesson and every girl in the room started to sigh. Oh, Belle, I think I'm in love."

Belle laughed. "I think your mama might have something to say about that."

Jo turned her twelve-year-old face Belle's way and replied, "We just won't tell her. How about that?"

Both girls laughed, then went downstairs for dinner.

SIX

LATER that same evening as Belle prepared for bed, Mrs. Best knocked lightly on Belle's partially open door, then asked, "Belle, may I speak with you?"

Belle answered affirmatively even though the pain of her father's fate still hung like weights on her heart and she didn't feel much like talking. She gestured Mrs. Best to a seat in one of the old stuffed chairs. Belle sat on the bed.

Silence slipped between them for a short while, then Mrs. Best said quietly, "You know, Belle, when my mother was sold, I didn't think the hurt would ever go away."

Belle looked up and met her kind brown eyes. "And did it?"

Mrs. Best shook her head. "No, but as time passed, I learned to manage it, as will you."

Belle bit her lip to keep the tears at bay. How would she live without her father? Mrs. Best said softly, "Something like this leaves a hole in your heart that will always be there."

Belle understood that. Her heart did feel wounded, and it was bleeding tears.

Mrs. Best then said, "Fugitives all over this nation have walked the path you're on. Like us, they've lost parents.

Some, their children. Facing freedom alone can be hard, but we survive. We have to, otherwise all the sacrifices made by those who came before us would be in vain."

Belle's tears were running freely down her cheeks.

"Belle, I know you're without family, but we'd be honored if you'd consider us your surrogate one. You're welcome here for as long as you wish."

Belle wondered what she'd done to deserve such special people in her life. "Thank you, Mrs. Best."

Mrs. Best took a clean handkerchief from the side pocket of her day gown and handed it to Belle. Belle wiped at her tears and blew her nose. She said finally, "Never knew one body could hold so many tears."

Mrs. Best smiled sadly. "It's a natural thing. No one will hold it against you if you cry for two months. Lord knows, I did."

"What was it like for you coming North?"

"Scary, strange—different. I'd never been in a place that had a real winter until I came North. Had no idea snow was so cold."

Belle gave her a watery smile.

"Then there was all the different types of people. I'd heard about free folks but had never met any, so when I got to Boston and learned there was a large community that dated back to before the Revolutionary War, I was speechless."

"I'd never met any free folks before coming here either."

"Then we have a lot in common, you and I."

"I suppose we do."

Belle looked into Mrs. Best's eyes and then asked, "Is it okay if I'm a bit scared of the future?"

"Yep."

"You said you were afraid when you first came."

"I was. Still am in many ways."

Belle hadn't expected that. "You don't seem afraid."

"I am, though. Afraid slavery will never end, and we'll have to live the rest of our lives fending off slave catchers. Michigan, like other states here in the North, has passed Personal Liberty Laws to protect folks like you and me against the horrid mandates of the Fugitive Slave Act, but they could be voided at any time depending on the political winds."

"I wish there'd been a law to protect my father."

"So do I."

"I know everyone did all they could to find him."

"Doesn't dull the hurt though, does it?"

Belle shook her head. "No, it doesn't."

Mrs. Best came over and took a seat beside Belle. "You're safe here. My family is now your family and we'll do whatever it takes to make certain you are as successful as you can be."

Belle still didn't understand such generosity. "But why are you doing this? You don't even know me."

"Sure I do. You're me, and every other soul who came North to find freedom. We must help each other if we are all to move forward."

Belle thought on that for a moment and decided that when she got the chance she, too would lend someone a helping hand.

Mrs. Best said, "It would be foolish to ask if this talk made you feel you better, because I know no amount of words can ease the hurt of losing your father, but I do hope I've set your mind at ease about the future."

Belle nodded. "You have."

Mrs. Best stood. "Good. Now, get some sleep. The hurt will dull, Belle, I promise."

"Thank you, Mrs. Best."

"You're welcome, dear. I'll see you in the morning."

She departed as quietly as she'd come.

As Belle lay in her bed she reflected back on the day. Learning her father's fate had been devastating—it seemed she'd carry the pain of his uncertain future for the rest of her life. Had she not been in such dire need, being comforted by Daniel would've been thrilling. Him holding her while she cried had made her feel so special, so cared about. She'd been embarrassed to the soles of her feet when Francine showed up, though, and Belle didn't need the ability to read to decipher the sneering, contemptuous look on the Queen's golden face. Belle hoped she hadn't made an enemy today. Mrs. Best's kind words had soothed her hurts, but Belle felt as if she'd been whipped about by a windstorm. She'd no idea where it would blow her or who she might be when everything settled, but she was surrounded by sterling examples of the person she could be. Content with that, Belle offered up one more prayer for her father's safety, then closed her eyes to sleep.

The next day, Belle placed her father's memory deep inside her heart and prepared to start her new life as a free young woman of color. To that end she planned to ask Mr. and Mrs. Best if it would be all right if she began taking in sewing and if they had any ideas as to how to drum up customers.

"Well, I need a dress for a ball next month. Maybe if I wear something you've created it would stir up interest," Mrs. Best replied as Belle and the family sat around the breakfast table.

Belle looked so surprised, everyone grinned.

Belle finally found speech. "Mrs. Best, I didn't mean

that I had to sew for you. I'm sure you have your own dressmaker. I—"

"Are you saying you *can't* make me a fancy gown or you *won't?*"

Belle studied her for a moment. "You would trust me to do that? Without even knowing if I can or not?"

"I've seen some of your work, dear. I trust you can do what you say you can."

Daniel said, "I could use a couple new shirts if you don't want to make Mama's gown."

Mr. Best asked, "Can you tailor suits, Belle?"

A wondrous Belle looked over at the grinning Jojo who said, "Guess you have your first customers, Belle."

Belle guessed she did.

After breakfast, Daniel drove Jojo to Trudy's house for school while Mr. Best headed out to his carpenter shop in the barn behind the house. That left Mrs. Best and Belle to see to the cleaning up, a job Belle didn't mind in the least.

"How about I wash today and you dry?" she asked her hostess.

"That's fine, then we can drag out some of my old *Godey's Lady's Books,* and see if we can't find a dress to make for me."

Since she'd been owned by a seamstress, Belle knew all about *Godey's Lady's Books.* Each issue had beautiful plates featuring the latest fashionable gowns and accessories. Because Belle couldn't read she paid little attention to the many articles on proper etiquette the magazine was also known for but devoured the well-done plates with their lovely dress designs.

"How about this one?" Mrs. Best asked Belle as they leafed through the pages of an issue.

Belle studied all the ruffles and flounces. "May I be truthful?"

"Of course."

"Well, you're tall, Mrs. Best, and all those ruffles and flounces will look silly on you. There was a lady back home. Mrs. Parly. She was tall, and I told her the same thing, but she knew better than me. So she made me sew it for her anyway. When she put it on, she looked like a Christmas tree."

Mrs. Best chuckled. "Then I will let you guide me."

Belle turned a few more pages, leafed through a few more issues, then said, "This is more you."

She handed it over. Mrs. Best scanned the clean lines and the stylishly done, lace-edged overdress and asked, "You can make something this beautiful?"

"Yes, ma'am. We just need to do your measurements, make the pattern and go buy the fabric and thread."

Mrs. Best looked over the plate again. "This is a lovely gown."

"Yes, it is. Mr. Best will think you're the prettiest lady at that ball."

Mrs. Best looked up with a smile. "Then I'm in your hands, Belle."

The two women spent the next hour talking about the dress and taking measurements. Although Belle couldn't read words, every seamstress had to be able to read numbers and she was no exception. On a piece of paper provided by Mrs. Best, Belle wrote down the measurements and did a rough calculation of how much fabric would be needed. "Now I need some butcher paper so I can make the pattern."

Mrs. Best didn't have any. "How about I have Daniel bring some home next time he goes into town?"

"That would be fine. When is the ball?"

Mrs. Best told her the date. It was over a month away.

Belle did some calculations in her head. "We should have plenty of time, then."

"Are you sure?"

Belle nodded. "Very sure."

"Then tomorrow or the next day, I'll have William take me to Detroit and I'll pick out the fabric. The Second Baptist Church down there has a Free Produce store."

"Then maybe after I finish your dress and you like it and your friends like it, too, I can save up enough money for a stitching machine."

"Sounds like a good way to go about it."

So that's what Belle planned to do.

She and Mrs. Best spent a few more moments talking about the various fabrics and color possibilities for the new gown, then cleaned up the mess of magazines and papers spread out on the floor of the parlor.

"Belle," Mrs. Best said as she headed for the kitchen, "Mr. Best and I are driving over to visit some friends in Ann Arbor this evening and we'll be back tomorrow afternoon. I'll start dinner later. I want you and Daniel to make certain Jo gets to bed at a reasonable hour."

"Yes, ma'am, but if you'll just tell me what you were going to prepare, I can cook the meal."

"No. Although I appreciate all your help around here, you're not a servant."

"But—"

"No buts. If you want to make yourself useful, go and take that tray in the kitchen out to the men. And tell William I said to show you the room."

Belle didn't think toting a tray a few feet would even begin to repay the Bests what she owed for taking her in, but she'd learned not to argue with Cecilia Best because the lady of the house always got her way. "You really ought to let me do more around here, you know."

"Young lady, if I did there'd be no need for me. You've helped with the cooking, the cleaning, the sweeping, the polishing. The wash."

Belle heard the praise in Mrs. Best's words and it warmed her insides. "I just wish to pay you back, and this is the only means I have."

"Well, William says if you work any harder we're going to have to pay you a salary, so stop it. At least wait until you get your own house."

Belle nodded. She really like Cecilia Best's wit. "Okay. I'll go and get the tray, but it isn't going to stop me from offering to help whenever I can."

Mrs. Best shook her head and said wistfully, "Oh, if only I had another son."

"What?"

"Nothing. Nothing. Go take the tray."

Belle had no idea what Mrs. Best was talking about, so she went to get the tray. Outside it was a bright and beautiful April day. The gentle breeze ruffled the hem of her old gray gown and blew softly against her brown cheeks. The tray in her hands held two steaming cups of coffee and a couple of man-sized wedges of last night's pound cake. It was the day's midmorning snack for the family's carpenters.

Belle liked the smells inside the large barn. The mixture of fragrant wood and oils pleasantly filled her nose the moment she entered. The spread-wide doors let in the sunlight, but the interior still caught and held shadows.

"Well, hello there, Miss Belle," Mr. Best called out from behind a long bench on the far right side of the barn. He had a plane in his hands and was working on what appeared to be a set of small doors. The wood was still pale and unfinished.

"Brought you coffee and cake," she called back.

Daniel, clad in a stained carpenter's apron over his shirt and trousers, looked up from where he stood over some stacked planks. Their eyes met and he asked, "Did you bring some for me?"

Belle tossed back, "Nope. Mr. Best and I are the only invitees to this party."

He grinned and felt his heart swell just looking at her. The old dress was too short for her tall, lean frame and the used shoes were scuffed, but the dark face with its long black lashes and sweetly curved lips made the hand-me-down garments inconsequential. She'd taken to wearing a long, thin ribbon around her soft, short hair, just like the one he'd seen in her hair that night up in her room. He liked that, too.

He also decided he liked her sassiness. "Well, if you think I'm going to let Papa have both pieces of that cake, you're mistaken."

"Oh, am I now?"

Belle knew Daniel would never return the feelings she had for him, so his friendship was her only option. It wouldn't be easy; her heart still skipped every time she saw him, but she didn't want to spend the rest of her life pining for something she'd never have.

The men went to the pump out back to rid themselves of the sawdust and grime, then each took a cup of coffee and a slice of cake from the tray.

"How're the chairs coming?" Belle asked Mr. Best.

Mr. Best was building an elaborate dining room set for a wealthy White couple in Toledo. The table had been shipped to them last week.

"They're almost done. One left to go."

Belle could see them up on the long trestle table near where he'd been working. They were made of a highly polished wood and gleamed even in the barn's dull light. She thought the table and chairs the most beautiful pieces of furniture she'd ever seen and hoped the new owners would appreciate the fine craftsmanship.

Mr. Best took a sip of his coffee and asked Belle, "What's my wife doing?"

"Preparing tonight's dinner. I volunteered to do it, but she turned me down. Says if I work any harder the family may have to pay me."

Mr. Best saluted Belle with his cup. "Cecilia's right. Though we do appreciate your willingness to help out."

Belle hazarded a look Daniel's way and found him watching her. Pulse beating, she hastily turned away. "She said something about you showing me a room?"

Seeking an explanation, Belle glanced between the two men who favored each other so much.

Mr. Best spoke. "Dani'll show you. There's something I need to talk to Cecilia about. I'll take this tray back up to the house."

He departed, and for the first time since Daniel held Belle in his arms the two young people were alone.

seven

AS the silence lengthened in the barn, Belle's nervousness increased. All she could think about was the last time they'd been together and how embarrassed she'd been when it ended. "I—want to apologize for getting you in hot water with your intended yesterday."

"There's no need," Daniel replied. "Francine understood how innocent it was."

Belle didn't believe that for a minute, but kept it to herself. "She's very beautiful, your Francine."

"Yes, she is."

Belle needed to change the subject. She didn't want to talk about Francine, nor did she want to remember the soft kiss Daniel had placed on her forehead while holding her, but the memory refused to stay buried. "Where's this room your mother wanted me to see?"

"Over here."

She followed him to the back of the barn, noting how smoothly he walked and how the muscles in his brown arms bulged above the rolled-up sleeves of his faded blue work shirt as he shoved aside a large pallet of wood that rested on the floor. Beneath the pallet lay a sawdust-covered tarp. He pulled it away to reveal a metal square set into the dirt. When he lifted the ring on the end of the square, Belle realized it was a door.

"Grab that lantern, would you?"

She handed him the lit lamp.

"Follow me," he said.

A marveling Belle walked over to the hole and looked in. She saw a narrow flight of wooden steps leading down into blackness.

"Watch your step," he cautioned.

Placing a hand on the cold, damp earth beside her, Belle slowly made her way down into what appeared to be a cellar. Once she stepped onto level ground and the light from the lamp cut through the underground darkness, she realized the space was more than just a cellar. There were two cots and a short, old-fashioned wood stove.

"This is where we hide fugitives," Daniel responded in answer to her unspoken question. "Took Papa, some of his friends and me almost a year to dig it out and shore it up. I thought we'd never get done hauling dirt back up to the surface."

Belle looked around the space and tried to imagine having to hide here until it was safe to move on to the next station. It wasn't big and neither was it cheery, but it wasn't slavery. "How many people have used this room?" she asked him.

"It's been here almost ten years, so probably hundreds. Multiply our visitors by the hundreds of others who've used stations across the country and you'll get thousands of runaways. The committee in Detroit boasts they've transported over thirty thousand folks to Canada since the mid forties alone."

Belle found that number amazing. "There are that many people escaping?"

He nodded.

Belle could only shake her head at the sheer size of what that represented. "Yet slavery continues."

"Yep."

When she met his eyes this time, their gazes held for what seemed to Belle to be an eternity. The lantern gave off just enough illumination to beat back the shadows, but even in the faint light, Daniel could see the smudge of mud she had on her cheek. "You have mud on your cheek."

Belle's hands went to her face. "Where?"

"Here," Daniel replied quietly, touching his finger to the spot, but he wasn't prepared for the tingling that resulted or for how soft her brown skin would feel. Seemingly of its own accord, that same finger stroked her cheek again.

Shaking, Belle looked up at him; she'd never had anyone touch her so delicately before. Her blood felt like it was rushing through her veins.

A different sort of silence rose between them then, one filled with unspoken questions and a sense of discovery still too new to recognize.

"Belle, I—"

"Dani! Is Belle down there with you?"

Mr. Best.

Unable to draw his eyes from Belle's, Daniel called back, "Yeah, Pa. She's right here."

"Your mother needs her. You two come on up."

"Okay."

Belle felt as if something had passed between them but she didn't know what to name it. The moment was over, however, maybe never to be visited again. "Thanks for showing me this place."

"You're welcome."

A few moments later, they were climbing to the surface and Belle was hurrying back to the house.

* * *

That same afternoon, before Mr. and Mrs. Best set off for their overnight visit with their friends, they called Belle downstairs. When she answered the summons, she saw that they were dressed and ready to go. Daniel was there at the door, too.

Mrs. Best pulled on her gloves. "Now, Belle, you and Daniel do your best to get Jojo to bed on time. Make sure her lessons are done before she starts experimenting with new hairstyles."

Belle smiled.

Mr. Best added, "There shouldn't be any visitors tonight, but if you do get a shipment you know what to do, son."

"Yes, Papa, I do."

Belle knew he meant fugitives. If anyone did arrive, she vowed to offer them as much assistance as she'd received in her time of need.

After verbal assurances from both Belle and Daniel that everything would be all right in their absence, Mr. and Mrs. Best left with a wave.

Daniel closed the door. "Well."

"Well," Belle echoed.

For a moment, neither could say more. The moment they'd shared in the underground room continued to play across both their minds.

Daniel, sensing Belle's nervousness matched his own, searched for a neutral topic. "I'll go pick up Jojo in an hour or so."

"That would be fine."

Daniel was attracted to Belle. He didn't want to admit it because of the long-standing assumption that he would marry Francine. In all the time he and Francine had been together he'd never even thought about another girl, but now…now this sixteen-year-old runaway with her spark-ling dark eyes and silk-smooth skin seemed to be under-mining that assumption.

"Is something wrong, Daniel?" Belle asked. He'd been gazing at her with such silent intensity she felt com-pelled to ask.

"No." It was a lie, of course, but in light of the com-mitments he'd already made, only a cad would further explore these unsettling new feelings. "I—have some cleaning up to do out in the barn. Will you be all right in here alone?"

Belle nodded. She seemed to have missed something but had no idea what it might've been. When he departed, Belle went up to her room.

Standing before her vanity mirror, Belle touched the spot on her cheek where his finger had brushed it and the rush through her blood returned. Did he see the same person she saw when she looked at herself in the mirror— a too-tall, sixteen-year-old girl with a dark-skinned face and average features? There was no way she'd ever have hair as long and glossy as Jojo's or Francine's, but she liked her short hair. It was the hair she'd been born with and it suited her, but what did Daniel see? Probably nothing, she told herself dejectedly as she turned away and picked up Jojo's almost-completed banner. She sat down in a chair and began putting the finishing touches on the Liberian flag. He probably saw nothing because he didn't even know she was alive, she wailed inwardly. The only reason he'd touched her cheek was because she'd had mud on it. She'd be willing to be Francine the Queen hadn't ever been caught with mud on her face like a dirty child. Determined to put Daniel Best out of her mind once and for all, Belle concentrated on her stitches.

* * *

Out in the barn, Daniel was putting away the tools and telling himself to quit thinking about Belle. He was supposed to be thinking about Francine. Francine was the one he planned to marry and raise a family with. He'd known her most of his life—he'd known Belle almost a month. The attraction made no sense, but he couldn't seem to convince his brain of that, or his feelings for that matter.

When he finished sweeping up and putting all the tools away, he closed the barn doors and went back up to the house. Taking a moment to wash up at the pump, he rid his hands, forearms and face of most of the sawdust and grime, then went inside. Belle was in the kitchen checking on the chicken his mother had left roasting for their dinner.

"How's it look?" he asked her.

She set the lid back on the roaster and slid it back into the stove. "By the time you get back with Jo it should be done."

She placed the oven pads and turned to face him. Once again she was struck by just how handsome Daniel Best really was. "Do you want biscuits or cornbread?"

"How about both?" he asked with a straight face.

She smiled in spite of herself. "No. One or the other."

"You're starting to sound a lot like my mother."

"I'll consider that a compliment," she said, inclining her head mockingly. "Now, which do you prefer?"

"Which one do you make the best?"

"Biscuits."

"Then biscuits it is. I'm on my way to fetch Jojo."

"Dinner will be waiting."

"Good, because I'm a hungry and growing man."

Belle smiled and watched him go. After his departure,

Belle found herself fantasizing how it might be to have Daniel for her husband and to be cooking dinner for them both. Telling herself she stood a better chance of seeing pigs crochet, she went to the pantry for the flour canister.

Belle had just gotten the biscuits rolled out and in the pan when she heard the sound of the door pull. She'd never been here alone before and never had to answer the door, so she hesitated. What if it was slave catchers? Convincing herself slave catchers wouldn't be so polite as to use the pull, she wiped her hands on her apron and hastened to the door. She did take a moment to look out of the window that gave a view of the porch. She saw two young men she didn't recognize.

The pull sounded again and Belle opened the door.

The two appeared to be about Daniel's age. Both were light skinned, tall and quite handsome. They favored each other enough to be twins.

One of the young men asked, "Are the Bests at home?"

Belle hesitated to give an answer without knowing if they were friend or foe. "May I ask why you're enquiring?"

"We have a box to deliver. We're the Morgans. Friends of Dani's."

Belle looked past them out to a wagon parked down by the road. True enough a large, rectangular-shaped crate rested in the bed. "Well, they're not here at the moment. Why don't you just leave it here on the porch?"

"Okay. My name's Jeremiah; this is my brother Adam."

"Pleased to meet you both. I'm Belle."

"You sure are," Jeremiah agreed, looking her over with an admiring smile and a playful light in his brown eyes.

The confusion on her face must've been plain, because Adam, the taller of the brothers, stated, "You must not speak French."

Belle admitted, "No, I don't."

"Well, in French, Belle means beautiful, and that you are. How long has Daniel been keeping you under wraps?"

Jeremiah added, "Better yet, does Francine the Queen know that a fairer beauty has entered the land?"

Belle couldn't help herself, she laughed. "Are you two always this incorrigible?"

"Only when faced with such a dazzling display of African loveliness."

Belle couldn't take it anymore. She held the door wide. "Come in before lightning strikes the house."

Laughing, both of the Morgans complied.

As it turned out, the two were longtime friends of the family. Both brothers had attended Oberlin with Daniel.

"Our parents are from Canada," Adam explained. "We moved here about ten years ago."

Jeremiah asked, "Where're you from, Belle?"

Before answering, Belle looked between the two. She didn't know if she could tell them the truth or if she was supposed to introduce herself as Mrs. Best's niece.

The sound of Jojo's happy voice emanating from the kitchen signaled Belle's deliverance. Jo and Daniel were back.

When Jojo entered the room, a smiling Jeremiah cracked, "Hello, pest."

Jojo grinned. "Hello, woodenhead. I see woodenhead two is with you, too."

Adam replied, "Don't you have some hair to curl somewhere? Where's your brother?"

"Right here," Daniel replied coming in behind his sister. He then turned to Belle and said, "We don't usually allow this kind of riffraff in the house."

"Hey!" Adam warned in mock protest. "How dare you defame me in front of this lovely ebony queen."

"Oh, Lord," Jojo said, rolling her eyes. "I'm going upstairs. Belle, you may wish to come, too."

Belle grinned. "I don't know, Jo. I kind of like being given a title." And she did. She was ebony, yes, but a lovely queen? Belle knew better, but enjoyed their good-natured teasing anyway. She then glanced Daniel's way to see if he was enjoying his friends' antics as much as she, but his jaw was tight, and the brown eyes viewing the brothers didn't look very friendly at all. *Whatever is the matter with him?* she wondered.

Jeremiah took one look at his face and asked, "What rocker rolled over your tail?"

His brother, gazing into Belle's eyes, chuckled. "Planned to keep this little jewel all to yourself, I'll bet, but you've already got Francine. This isn't the Bible; you don't get two."

Belle dropped her head to hide her grin. She liked the Morgan brothers very much.

Daniel asked them, "Did you come over here for a reason?"

"We've a crate outside for you."

"What kind of crate?" Daniel asked.

Adam used his hands to intimate his words. "A very big crate."

"Where's it from?"

"Philadelphia, I think. We were at the train station today to send off a parcel for Mama when one of the porters asked if we knew a William Best. We said yes, so he asked that we deliver it. Says it's from William Still."

"William Still?!" Daniel exclaimed. "Oh, Jesus! Come on!"

To everyone's surprise, Daniel ran out the front door.

Daniel was already up on the wagon bed when the others came out to join him. He was silently praying, too, but no one knew that. Daniel saw that small holes had been drilled in the side of the crate and that gave him hope. He placed his ear against the wood and listened. Silence. Knowing his parents would want him to remain calm, he told Adam, "Quick, get in and drive this thing behind the house. Jere, there are tools right inside the barn door. I need a claw hammer and a crowbar. Run. I want to get this opened as soon as we get there. Jo, help him."

Jeremiah and Jojo both took off at a run.

Belle, seeing the grimness on Daniel's face but having no idea of the cause, asked, "Is there anything I can do?"

"Yes, pray. Pray that the person in here is still alive."

He turned to Adam. "Let's go, but take it easy."

As the wagon headed for the back of the house, Belle followed it, too stunned to speak.

Adam stopped the wagon behind the barn so it couldn't be seen from the road, and as Belle and Jojo watched, Daniel and the Morgan brothers used the claw hammers and the crowbar to loosen the nailed-down lid of the crate. Belle did indeed pray. Anyone desperate enough to ship themselves this way deserved to live.

Inside they found a bearded, middle-aged, dark-skinned man, lying in fetid, foul-smelling straw, but his body was so still, it was impossible to determine whether he was alive.

A concerned Daniel knelt and placed his fingertips against the man's neck. The pulse, although faint, was steady. "He's alive."

Relief filled Belle and the others.

Adam asked, "Is he asleep?"

Daniel shook the body gently, first once and then again. "Doesn't seem like it. Maybe took some type of medicine to make him sleep."

Daniel shook him again. Still nothing. "Okay, let's take him up to the house. I don't think Mama would want him to be put in the hidey-hole, not while he's like this."

Belle agreed. It would probably terrify the man to awaken and find himself underground alone and unable to remember how he'd come to be there. She knew it would scare her to death.

"How about I ride over and get Bea once we get him inside?" Jeremiah offered.

Daniel nodded. "Good idea, but let's see if we can get our guest on his feet. Adam, go out front and make sure nobody's lurking."

He hurried off. The last thing they needed were spying slave catchers.

Jeremiah and Daniel managed to get the unconscious man between them and threw his arms over their necks. His head lolled forward uselessly and the toes of his worn brogans dragged on the ground, but they were able to get him to the house.

"Let's put him in my room for now," Daniel suggested in a voice strained by the man's weight. Adam grabbed the fugitive's legs and the three young friends maneuvered up the stairs. When they reached the landing, Jojo ran ahead and retrieved a tarp from the chest in her parents' room to place over Daniel's sheets, then they gently deposited their charge onto the bed. He lay there as unmoving as he had been in the crate.

"What now?" Adam asked.

"Go and get Bea Meldrum; maybe she can figure out what's ailing him or how to make him wake up."

So Adam left. Daniel pulled a quilt over the man, then he and the others went back downstairs.

Belle said, "I hope Mrs. Meldrum can help him."

"I do, too," Daniel replied.

The dinner forgotten for now, they all sat down to wait for Adam to return with Bea.

eight

ONCE the white-haired Bea arrived she hastened upstairs. Seated on the bed, she felt the temperature of the man's forehead, then eased back the lids of his eyes. "He's been drugged," she determined. "With what, I don't know. It hasn't killed him, so I suppose all we can do is wait until he comes around."

The straw he'd been lying in had been fouled by bodily fluids, and he didn't smell very pleasant. Bea noticed it, too. She waved a hand in front of her nose. "He's pretty pungent. You want me to wash him up?"

Daniel nodded. "If you don't mind."

She smiled knowingly. "Get me a basin and towels."

So while Jojo went off to fetch what Bea needed, the rest went back downstairs to wait.

A while later, Bea made her way back downstairs, and Daniel asked her, "How is he?"

"Still asleep, but cleaner."

"Do you think he'll pull through?" Belle asked.

Bea shrugged. "Hard to tell, but he's got a strong pulse and he doesn't seem to be in any kind of physical distress. All we can do is wait."

Jeremiah asked, "Do you want me and Adam to take you back now, or do you wish to stay until he awakens?"

Bea answered, "I think I'll go on home. There's no telling how long he'll be out. When will your folks be back, Dani?"

"Tomorrow afternoon."

"Then you should be all right until then. You've managed freight before."

Daniel nodded. He also had Belle and Jojo's help. He doubted anything would arise that the three of them couldn't handle.

Bea added, "But if he hasn't awakened by, say, tomorrow this time, come and get me."

"I will. Thanks for your help."

"You're welcome."

Bea then looked around at the faces of the young people filling the small parlor, and said, "You all did real well. The Vigilance Committee will be proud."

The group basked in her praise.

Moments later, Adam and Jeremiah gave Belle departing bows, then escorted Bea out to their wagon.

Hoping it might brighten the air, Belle asked, "Does anyone want dinner?"

Daniel and Jojo nodded affirmatively, so Belle headed to the kitchen while Jojo and Daniel set the table. As they ate, conversation was sparse. The food was excellently prepared but no one felt much like eating. Their minds were on the unconscious man upstairs.

After the table was cleared, Daniel decided he'd sit with the man awhile in case he awakened, even though Belle volunteered. He told her, "It'll probably be safer if I do it. We don't know who he is. I don't want to find out too late that I put you in harm's way."

He was holding her eyes and Belle felt as if she were

drowning in them. She somehow managed to nod her understanding but found herself incapable of looking away.

Jojo took this in for a moment, then bent and peered first at her brother's face and then at the face of her friend. She waved a hand between them. When they both started as if awakened, Jojo said approvingly, "Well, now."

Daniel looked her way. Voice and face filled with brotherly irritation, he asked, "What?"

Jojo shook her head innocently. "Nothing. I'm going up to do my studies now. See you later, Belle."

Belle thought Jojo's pleased expression was very reminiscent of the knowing look Mrs. Best wore the day she and Francine found Daniel holding Belle in his arms. Belle wanted to know what the look meant, if anything, and decided to have a talk with Jojo later.

Daniel, on the other hand, knew that the more he stayed around Belle, the less he thought about Francine. "I should go and see how the guest is faring," he told Belle stiffly. "I'll see you later."

That said, he left.

Belle thought his departure so abrupt, she wondered if she'd said or done something wrong. She couldn't recall anything, so she decided whatever was bothering him must have been caused by something else.

Upstairs in his room, Daniel drew the drapes to close out the early evening sky and turned down the lone lamp. He then took a seat on one of his bedroom chairs. Their visitor was still asleep. The committee would want to interview him once he awakened so they could determine who he was and where he wanted to relocate. Daniel didn't think his parents had been expecting such a uniquely packaged runaway, otherwise they wouldn't have gone visiting. The crate's sender, Mr. William Still, was one of the most famous conductors on the Underground Railroad. His station in Philadelphia had been visited by thousands of runaways and his knowledge of most of the other conductors nationwide made him a conduit not only for fugitives but for the dissemination of news and information relevant to the abolitionist struggle. Jere and Adam were owed a tremendous thanks. Were it not for them, the man might've died, never knowing he'd made it to freedom.

In the shadowy silence the man's rhythmic snoring sounded even and strong, so Daniel picked up one of the many newspapers at the foot of his nightstand to pass the time. He glanced over an editorial summarizing the views of Mr. Abraham Lincoln, a contender for the presidency, but Daniel couldn't concentrate; Belle kept floating across his mind. Jere and Adam were his best friends and well-known for their success with the ladies, but Daniel hadn't liked them spinning their smiles around Belle. He doubted she'd ever encountered anyone as smooth as those two, and he didn't want her to be hurt by their flirting ways. Or at least that was what he told himself. A more honest assessment would center on jealousy, but even though he'd already admitted his attraction to her, he wasn't ready to own up to jealousy. At least not yet.

Had she ever had a beau, though? he wondered. As shy as she was, he tended to doubt it. He knew that many female captives were already breeding by the time they were Belle's age, and because importing new slaves had been banned since 1807, slave women were often forced into having more and more babies. Was that one of the reasons she and her father had escaped? Daniel couldn't imagine his sister having to face such a future.

He was glad she'd never have to and as long as they kept Belle safe, neither would she.

A few hours later, Belle knocked softly on Daniel's partially closed door and stuck her head around it. "How's our guest doing?" she asked.

Daniel, seated in the soft, shadowy light, set his newspaper aside. "Still asleep." He never remembered being so elated by one girl's presence before. He wanted her to come closer and maybe sit with him while he waited for the man to awaken but knew it wouldn't be proper for her to do so.

This was the first time Belle had ever seen the interior of Daniel's room. Jojo was right. He certainly did have a lot of books. Dark wood shelves lined the walls. Belle could see him watching her, and as usual it left her a bit flummoxed. Proper young women weren't supposed to visit a gentleman's bedroom; she knew that, but she thought it might be all right if she stood here by the door, just for a moment or two. To cover her nervousness, she asked, "Is escaping in a box common?"

Daniel knew why she was choosing to stand in the doorway. Although her innocence touched him, he answered her question in a serious tone. "Not really, though it has been done a few times. First one I heard of was Henry Brown back in the forties. Folks call him Box Brown now. Shipped himself from Richmond to Philadelphia. Caused such a stir folks wrote songs about it."

"Really?"

"Yep."

Belle echoed Daniel's earlier thoughts, "Good thing the Morgans were at the station."

Daniel nodded. "It might have been days before we knew the man was there. I'll bet the letter Mr. Still sent my father alerting him of this arrival won't get here until next week sometime."

Even a former slave like Belle knew how notoriously slow the mail could be.

"Well," Daniel said, "he made it—that's what counts, and in one piece."

Silence slipped between them then. He couldn't take his eyes off her and she couldn't look away.

Belle finally found the words to say, "Jo and I are going to do some sewing. If you need me, call me."

"I will."

"I'll look in on you later."

"That would be fine."

Long after her departure, Daniel was still smiling.

The man in Daniel's bed awakened at half past ten. He struggled to sit up. Noticing Daniel, he froze, then his wary eyes swept the unfamiliar surroundings.

"You're safe," Daniel reassured him.

The runaway tried to say something, but the words came out as a hoarse whisper.

Belle, who'd just come into the room to see if Daniel needed anything, quickly poured some water into a cup from the pitcher she'd left on the nightstand earlier. She offered the fugitive the cup, but his hand shook so badly she had to guide the vessel to his lips. "Slowly," she cautioned.

His hands around her own were clammy and cold, but she set aside the unpleasant feel because he needed assistance. When he'd taken another few swallows, he nodded at Belle, then wearily dropped back against the pillows.

Daniel asked, "What's your name?"

"Parker—Nelson Parker. Where am I?" he croaked softly.

"Michigan."

His eyes widened and he bolted upright. "Michigan!"

Daniel had a curious look on his face. "Yes."

The man slumped back against the bedding, then began angrily pounding his fists on the mattress. Tears streamed unashamedly down his bearded cheeks. As if deeply grieved, his head rolled slowly back and forth upon the pillow, and he whispered hoarsely, "Oh, Lily, why? Why?"

Belle looked over at Daniel. He appeared to be as concerned by the man's demonstration as she.

Daniel asked, "What's wrong, sir?"

As if talking to himself, the man replied tightly, "She knew I wouldn't leave without her." He beat his fists against the bed again once more, then to their surprise tried to get to his feet. "I have to go back—"

Daniel rushed forward. "Whoa, whoa. Hold on a minute, friend. You're in no condition to go anywhere."

The man's attempts to push Daniel aside might've been effective before he'd come North, but being confined and drugged had left him so weak Jojo could've kept him in bed. Realizing that seemed to drain him completely. Seated on the edge of the bed he hung his head and began to sob as if his heart had broken.

Belle had seen only one other man cry so emotionally before: her father. He had cried just like this the day her mother was sold. Having his beloved Sara torn from his life had left her father even more bitter toward slavery. Nelson Parker brought thoughts of her missing father rushing back.

Daniel ventured forward. "Friend, is there anything we can do?"

"Yes," he declared brusquely. "Send me home."

Daniel's lips tightened. "How about we talk about that after you get your strength back?"

Daniel handed the man a clean handkerchief. He made use of it, then slowly crawled back beneath the quilts. He turned his back on them and didn't utter another word.

Outside the closed door, Daniel huddled with Belle and Jojo. "I guess we'll have to wait to hear our guest's full story. He seems real torn up, though. Hope he doesn't try and leave."

"He's too weak to make it across the room," Belle said.

Daniel agreed. "You're probably right, but I think we ought to keep a close eye on him anyway."

Jojo said, "I can take a turn."

Daniel shook his head. "Both of you are going to bed."

Belle asked, "But what if you need something from the kitchen?"

"Then I'll just walk down and get it."

"Daniel—"

"Belle—"

She smiled. He did, too.

Daniel then said genuinely, "You've both been a real help today, but time to go to bed. There'll be more to do tomorrow."

Jojo pouted mockingly. "Okay, but if I'm needed, come get me."

"I will," he replied.

Jojo asked Belle, "Do you believe him?"

Belle tossed back, "Not for a minute."

Daniel grinned. Two weeks ago she would've never given him such a saucy reply. It was as if she'd finally become comfortable enough in her new surroundings to let her true nature rise and show itself. He sensed she was still shy, but not as much as he'd initially believed.

Jojo went into her room, but Daniel's voice stopped Belle. "Belle."

She turned back. "Yes?"

"Thanks for all your help."

Buoyed by his praise, Belle replied, "Glad I could. If you wish to sleep later, I can come and sit with him."

"That won't be necessary. I'll be fine in the chair. I've also a pallet under the bed I can pull out if need be."

"Are you sure?"

Daniel nodded. He searched his mind for something else to talk about so that she'd stay and talk with him a bit longer but knew he shouldn't keep her. "I'll see you later then."

"Good night," she told him.

"Night, Belle," Daniel answered. "See you in the morning."

Belle gave Daniel one last look from beneath her lashes, then headed to her room.

Lying in bed, Belle thought about Nelson Parker. She wondered what his story was. He'd seemed truly distraught. Had he been sent to freedom against his will? Belle couldn't imagine wanting to go back now that she'd had a taste of what freedom was all about. She'd had no idea just how limited her life had been as a slave until the Bests entered her life, yet the man down the hall hadn't seemed happy to learn he was no longer a captive. She wondered if he knew that here one could be oneself; that you no longer had to keep your eyes lowered or speak only when spoken to. Belle could look folks in the eye and voice her thoughts without fear of reprisal. She could come and go. Having the chance to do something besides be hunched over a needle all day, she found every day to be a new experience. It occurred to her that now that she was settling into this new life, maybe the time had come to start exercising those parts of herself she wished to explore, to shed the invisible shackles slavery had forced her to wear and begin to build the person she wanted to become. She could be as poised as Mrs. Best or as confident as Jojo. Given time, she could be just about anyone she chose to be. The contented Belle was still mining the possibilities as she drifted off to sleep.

nine

The next morning, Daniel got up early and quietly tiptoed out of the room so he wouldn't awaken Mr. Parker. Daniel had grown accustomed to having a cup of coffee to start the day, but because his mother was away he had to make it himself. To his surprise, Belle was already in the kitchen laying bacon into a hot skillet. He saw that she'd made another batch of her heavenly biscuits to go with the grits and eggs also waiting to be prepared.

A confused Daniel asked, "How long have you been up?"

"Since five."

He stared as if she'd suddenly grown another head. "Five?!"

Belle nodded. "It's the time I got up at home. Mrs. Grayson wanted her breakfast served promptly at quarter past six every morning, so I'm accustomed to rising early. Of course, your mama won't let me do this when she's here, but since she isn't—"

Daniel smiled his understanding.

"Coffee's already done."

Daniel thought her an angel. "Thank you." He yawned, pouring himself a cup. "Have you seen the pest this morning?"

Belle smiled. "Not yet."

Daniel took a small sip of the hot brew and found it delicious. "Don't tell Mama, but this coffee is much better than hers."

Belle began placing her biscuits in the pan. "It's not nice to lie so early in the morning, Daniel Best."

He chuckled. "I'm not lying."

Belle rolled her eyes. "I'll bet you'll tell that to any girl who'll listen."

He stared. "Belle?"

She paused and looked up. "What?"

"Where'd all this sassiness come from?"

She rolled out the remaining scraps of dough. "What sassiness?"

"That sassiness."

"It's not sassiness; it's just me."

"Then what happened to the shy, quiet girl who was here a few days ago?"

"She's still here. I've just been feeling my way, that's all. Learning the lay of the land, as they say. And—since it looks pretty good, I decided to start being me."

Daniel found this side of her so intriguing he didn't know if he was ready for the real Belle; he had enough trouble handling the old one.

The biscuits were all in the pan now and she popped them into the oven. "Well?" she asked, turning to face him.

Over his cup, he asked in return, "Well, what?"

"Is it all right for me to be me, or at least who I'm trying to be?"

He paused and looked into her eyes. The seriousness reflected there moved him. "Yes, it's okay."

She smiled. "Good. I hope the world's ready."

Daniel chuckled. "Me, too."

Since the day was Saturday and there was no school, Jojo slept in. While Belle saw to the cooking, Daniel took a few more draws on his coffee, then asked, "When did you decide you wanted to be someone else?"

Belle paused, and thought on that for a moment, then said, "I don't think I'm being someone else. I think I'm turning into the me I couldn't be as a slave."

"What do you mean?"

"I couldn't speak my mind, look people in the eye— things of that nature. But here I can, can't I?" It was more statement than question.

"Yes, you can."

"And when I'm done growing myself, I want to be as confident as your sister and as polished and wise as your mother."

Daniel laughed. "You'll be some kind of woman then."

Belle smiled. "I would be, wouldn't I?"

He shook his head with amusement. "Yes, you would." And every eligible bachelor in the county would be lined up at the door, wanting her favors, Daniel noted to himself. That realization didn't sit well.

Once the biscuits were done, Belle asked, "Are you going to eat down here, or upstairs?"

Daniel looked at the bacon, eggs and grits and knew the answer. "Here. Mr. Parker was asleep when I left. I'm hoping he'll stay that way for a bit, so let's eat."

They sat at the dining table in the parlor. After a few moments of silent eating, Belle asked, "Is the food okay?"

He nodded. The fat, light-as-air biscuits were also better than his mother's, another truth he decided he'd keep to himself.

"Is your Francine a good cook?" Belle asked then.

Francine couldn't boil water, but being the loyal intended, Daniel lied. "She's a wonderful cook."

"That's good, since you seem to like to eat."

He shot her an amused look. "All right, Miss Belle, there's sassy and then there's sassy."

"There's also truth, Daniel Best. Save your sister at least one of those biscuits."

Daniel smiled guiltily. He'd eaten at least five. "I'm a growing man."

"With a hollow stomach."

They both laughed, each enjoying this time together.

Moments later, an obviously sleepy Jojo came dragging into the room, plate in hand. She was dressed in her night-clothes and robe. "It's far too early to be so happy," she declared, taking a seat. "I could hear you two on the stairs. Good morning."

"Good morning," they replied.

Having finished his breakfast, Daniel backed his chair from the table and stood. "I should get back."

"Leave your plate," Belle told him. "I'll take it to the kitchen when I take mine." She wondered if this was how he and Francine would spend their mornings once they were married.

"Okay. I'll see you both later."

And he was gone.

Nelson Parker awakened around noon. When his eyes met Daniel's he said, "I thought I dreamed you. Guess I didn't."

"No, sir." Daniel wondered how the man would react now.

"That's twice you've called me that."

"What?"

"Sir. Never had anyone call me that before. What's your name?"

"Name's Daniel. I was raised to be respectful of my elders," Daniel replied.

"I understand, but folks like me don't get much of that where I'm from."

Daniel watched Nelson struggle to a sitting position, then asked him, "Where are you from?"

"Richmond."

Daniel found that surprising. "You've come far."

"Too far."

Nelson Parker quieted then as if seeing rising memories. "Having dinner with her was the last thing I remember. She must've put something in my food to make me sleep."

He turned his head to meet Daniel's eyes, and Daniel asked, "Who?"

"My wife, Lily. She knew I wouldn't come North without her. I gave her no choice, I guess."

Daniel had no idea what the man was talking about, but from the tone of Parker's voice, he sensed the runaway loved Lily very much. It reminded Daniel of how his father sounded sometimes when speaking of his mother, Cecilia—as if his sun rose and set in her smile. "Did your wife send you North?"

"I'm assuming. Her and her mother. Both of them wanted me to run, but how could I, knowing I'd have to leave them behind?"

"Why was that?"

"Lily's mother's sick. Bedridden. Been like that a long time. Her master was decent enough to keep Lily on the place to take care of her, but not enough to free them."

"So how'd you wind up in a box?"

He paused for a moment. "What box?"

"Mr. Still shipped you here from Philadelphia in a big crate."

Nelson's eyes widened, but before he could react further, Belle entered the room carrying a tray bearing Daniel's lunch.

Belle was pleased to find their visitor awake and alert. "Good afternoon, Mr. Parker."

He nodded, then said, "Just knew I'd dreamed you, too."

Belle shook her head. "Nope. I am real as life. My name's Belle. How are you?"

"Feeling a mite better, Belle. That food sure smells good."

"Well, how about you take this plate and I'll bring Daniel another?"

Even though Belle knew how much Daniel liked to eat, under the circumstances she doubted he'd mind having Mr. Parker's needs satisfied first, especially since there was plenty more food in the kitchen.

As Belle settled the tray across Parker's lap, he asked, "You sure you got enough to spare?"

Belle nodded. "Yes. Now, eat up, but start slow. How long has it been since you've eaten?"

"What's today?"

Daniel answered, "Saturday."

"Went to visit Lily on Sunday." He paused for a moment as if trying to verify his memories. "Yes, Sunday. Had dinner, then I turned up here. It's what I get for loving a healer woman."

He spooned up some stew, and as he swallowed, said, "Lord, this is good. Son, you're a lucky man to have a lady who can cook like this."

Embarrassment scorched Belle from her forehead to her toes. "I'm not his lady," she offered.

Nelson looked between the two, then asked Daniel, "Why not? You waiting for someone to beat you to her?"

Belle chuckled at the stunned look on Daniel's face, then explained, "He already has an intended."

Parker shot off another question. "Can she cook like this?"

Daniel stuttered, "No—I mean yes."

His fractured answer drew Belle's immediate attention and Daniel looked guilty. Did that mean that Francine couldn't cook? The knowledge made Belle smile inside. "Daniel, I'll get you another plate. Be right back."

After her departure, Parker said to Daniel, "She's a nice girl. I apologize for putting you on the spot that way. Just assumed—"

"It's quite all right, Mr. Parker. I'm sure Belle didn't take offense either."

"Well, if I didn't love my Lily, and I was ten years younger, I'd give these bucks around here a run for their money. Like my women tall and dark like that."

Daniel didn't know what to say. He was finding himself attracted to tall and dark, too.

Parker said, "Now, finish telling me about this box."

So Daniel did, adding the vital role played by the Morgan brothers.

"Owe those two my life, I guess."

Daniel thought so, as well, then asked, "You don't really wish to return South, do you?"

"Yes, I do, but truth is, I can't. Not now, and Lily knew that. If I go back, there's no telling what'll happen to me."

Daniel understood. Few, if any, masters welcomed their escaped slaves back home with open arms. Parker could be whipped or at worst killed for his actions. "So what will you do?"

Parker shrugged, "Make my life somewhere here, I suppose, then try and figure how to get Lily freed, too."

"Do you think you can buy her freedom?"

"Don't know."

"Well, my parents and I are members of the local Vigilance Committee. I'm sure we can help you figure it all out."

Parker responded the same way Belle had when she first arrived. "What's a vigilance committee?"

So for the next little while, Daniel explained to Parker how the committee worked and what it stood for. He told him about the rallies and the speeches, the debates and how the abolitionist communities of all races agitated for the freedom of the country's three million slaves. "Some committees have had armed confrontations with slave catchers and others have gone into courtrooms and forcibly removed fugitives from the witness stand to keep them from being returned to slavery."

Parker's bearded face showed he'd been impressed. "Lots going on up here in the North."

"Yes, there is, and it won't stop until slavery's stopped."

"Amen."

Late that same afternoon, Mr. and Mrs. Best returned home. They were surprised to hear of Nelson Parker's arrival and immediately went up to speak with him. A short while later, Mrs. Best came back down, leaving her husband and Daniel to continue the in-depth interview the committee members conducted with every passenger who passed through their station. Belle knew that many of the questions would be some of the same ones put to her. Questions concerning her past; how she'd been treated; who owned her; and how many years she'd been held against her will. In Mr. Parker's case the subject of relocation would be discussed also.

The next morning, Mr. Parker was gone. He'd been

passed on to another station; Belle didn't know where but put him in her prayers, right behind her father.

For the next few days, Belle poured all of her energies into working on the pattern for Mrs. Best's gown. Daniel had gotten the butcher paper for her, and once the pattern was measured and cut, she began pinning the paper pieces to the fabric, a beautiful burgundy sateen Mrs. Best found in Detroit at historic Second Baptist's Free Produce store. Belle was so focused on making this the best gown she'd ever created, she spent all of her free time working. Sewing was Belle's love, her passion, and now that she had an opportunity to take it up again, it was hard to concentrate on anything else.

The next day, Francine paid the Bests a visit.

It seemed Francine was giving a mind feast—whatever that was. Belle refused to show her ignorance by asking to have the particulars of the event explained; she didn't want to give Francine the satisfaction. Belle looked to Jojo and Mrs. Best, who were also in the parlor. Jojo looked cool, her normal stance whenever Francine came around. Mrs. Best's face gave away nothing, but her eyes were as cool as her daughter's.

"Please say you'll come, Belle."

Francine was dressed in gray today: gray dress, cape, hat and shoes. Her long glossy hair was parted simply and coiled on her neck. Once again, Belle could see why Daniel wanted to marry her. "I don't know, Francine. I'm really busy—"

"Oh, pooh. It can't be that important. Everyone wants to meet you."

As if she'd anticipated resistance, Francine then announced, "And Belle, you can't use the excuse that you've nothing to wear. My girlfriends and I went through our trunks and found you some things."

For the first time, Belle noticed the large black carpetbag sitting at Francine's tiny, well-shod feet. Francine picked it up and thrust the bag at Belle, giving her no choice but to take it. Belle didn't mind charity, after all she had very few personal possessions, but having Francine aid her didn't make her feel grateful in the least. In fact she felt like a penniless, ill-dressed runaway having to take her better's hand-me-downs. "Thank you, Francine. I'm sure I'll find something suitable in here. Please give your friends my thanks."

Francine smiled like a fox closing in on a chicken. "I will. The party's at my home on Saturday. I can trust you to ride over with Dani, can't I? You aren't going to need more comforting again, are you?"

"I'll do my best to keep my needs in check."

Francine raised a perfectly arched eyebrow at Belle's small show of backbone and declared, "Please see that you do."

Out of the corner of her eye, Belle saw the smile on Jojo's face.

Francine then looked to Jojo and said, "Is your brother out in the barn?" Jojo nodded.

"Then be a plum and go tell him I'm here."

"Tell him yourself."

Her mother snapped warningly, "Josephine, go and get your brother."

Jojo dragged herself off the sofa. "Yes, ma'am."

Since Belle had no desire to watch Daniel and Francine bill and coo, she said to Mrs. Best, "Is there anything you need help with in the kitchen?"

Mrs. Best smiled. "As a matter of fact, I do. Jojo's been raving about your biscuits. Show me how they're made."

Belle could've kissed Jojo's mama for boosting her spirits. "Of course. Lead the way. Good-bye, Francine."

"I'll see you soon, Belle."

It sounded like a warning, but Belle shrugged it off, blaming it on her imagination.

Belle didn't get a chance to view the contents of the carpetbag until later that evening. She and Jojo were sequestered in Belle's room working on Mrs. Best's gown; rather, Belle was working, Jojo was still sputtering about Francine's visit.

"I still don't see why Daniel wants to marry her."

"Obviously he sees something there," Belle said in an attempt to be charitable, even though she personally thought the girl a snake.

Jo asked, "What did those dresses of hers look like? I bet they're hideous."

"I don't know," Belle replied, setting aside one of the gown's sleeves. "Haven't had time to look."

Belle dug the first few out of the bag. Jojo was correct: they were hideous. Most were at least two inches too short and far too small across the middle. None were even close to new. "She knows you're at least four inches taller than she is; why would she pick those?" Jojo asked critically.

It was quite plain Francine wanted Belle to be the most ridiculously attired person at her affair. The rest of the gowns were no better. Belle wished she hadn't agreed to attend the party.

Mrs. Best walked in then. Seeing the dresses lying across the bed, she asked, "Any of them suitable?"

Jojo cracked, "Only if you want Belle to be a laughing-stock."

Mrs. Best scanned the offerings. One had a badly frayed hem; another she picked up had torn seams beneath the badly stained underarms. "If her mother, Dessa, were alive she'd take a buggy whip to that girl's behind for sending you these rags."

"It's all right, Mrs. Best. I wasn't really wanting to go in the first place."

"No, it isn't, and yes, you did, and even if you didn't want to go, you should. It's time you were around people your own age."

Belle looked over the dresses again. "You know, if I put this bodice on this dress—"

An epiphany resonated through Belle like a thunderclap. She looked to Jojo and said excitedly, "Hand me those scissors."

ten

It took Belle a day and a half, and she was up most of Friday night, but by the time Saturday evening rolled around, she'd created a dress worthy enough to be worn anywhere. Using various pieces of this one and the lace and sleeves of that one, Belle put together a dress so uniquely fashionable it was hard to imagine it had come from rags.

"My goodness!" Mrs. Best gushed once she got a look at Belle all dressed up. "You look wonderful."

"Thank you."

Jojo had curled Belle's short hair and draped a ribbon around her head that matched the lovely, dark blue gown. The hooped petticoat borrowed from Mrs. Best gave the dress a subtle fullness. The new black slippers, given to her as a gift from Mr. and Mrs. Best, brought tears to Belle's eyes. Now, looking at herself in the mirror, Belle felt like a dark-skinned princess. She'd never, ever worn such finery before. Never. It amazed her that the confident-looking young woman staring back at her was actually her. Less than two months ago, she'd been a slave, and now... "This is the first dress I've ever made for myself."

Mrs. Best came over and gave her shoulder a short hug. "May it be the first of dozens, my dear. You're going to need a club to beat back the young men."

"Do you think so?"

"I know so."

Belle had butterflies in her stomach all of a sudden. "I don't know anything about talking to young men. What if they want to know where I'm from?"

"I'm sure everyone in Daniel's set knows all about your circumstances, and they'll be respectful."

Belle didn't know if she believed that or not. She wasn't ashamed of her past, but she didn't want to be whispered about or pointed at either.

Mrs. Best seemed to read her mind. "Just put on your confidence and hold your head high. You'll be fine, you'll see."

Belle hoped she was right.

When it was time to depart, Bell found Daniel waiting in the parlor. Her entrance made him turn away from the conversation he'd been having with his father, and she saw his eyes go wide. He seemed speechless, so Mr. Best offered up, "What my son is trying to say is, you look very lovely, Belle."

"Thank you, Mr. Best."

Daniel wondered how long it would take for his heart to start beating again. Belle looked radiantly confident yet shy. One would never believe this well-dressed young woman to be the same girl he'd had to carry upstairs because she'd walked her feet raw. He finally found his voice. "My father's right, Belle. You look—fine."

"Thank you, Daniel."

Daniel couldn't help himself. He stared and stared so long, Belle finally asked, "Are you ready to go?"

He shook himself. "Um—yes." He gestured her to the door. "Shall we?"

Belle left the room. Daniel took a moment to look back at his father and saw a smile in his eyes.

His father said, "Have a good time."

"We will."

Once Belle and Daniel were under way, Belle admitted, "I'm a bit nervous about this."

"About what?"

"Going to Francine's party. What is a mind feast, anyway?"

"A real mind feast has food and things for the mind: like a lecturer or an author. Sometimes money is raised for the Cause, or for a fugitive family in need, but Francine's is just an excuse for her friends to get together and have a good time."

Belle hazarded a look his way. "I see. Pardon me if I'm speaking out of turn, but you sound like you don't approve."

"Truthfully, Belle? I don't. Mind feasts serve a legitimate purpose—they're special, honored. They're not supposed to be the setting for parlor games and gossip."

"It might be fun."

"That's my point: it's not supposed to be fun."

Belle chuckled. "Oh, Daniel, are you always so serious?"

"Yes." He glanced away from the road a moment to look her way. "It's who I am. Is it so wrong?"

Belle searched his eyes, then slowly shook her head. "No, it isn't," she reassured him softly. "But you're free, Daniel; you should enjoy it sometimes."

As if he were thinking over what she'd said, he didn't

speak for a moment, then offered, "Never thought about it in those terms before."

"It is a different way of looking at it, I know, but from where I sit, freedom is too wonderful not to spend some of it having fun. Or am I wrong?"

"No, you're not wrong. I guess having been a slave gives you a different outlook on things. You haven't had much fun in your life, have you?"

"Nope. Started sewing when I was little and been doing that all my life. My mistress frowned on me going to any of the social events the planters sometimes let their slaves have, like on Christmas or New Year's. She wanted me to believe the folks I'd meet would be bad influences; said she didn't want those influences to rub off on me and offend her customers."

Daniel shook his head. "Then we have to make sure you have some fun at Franny's."

"No, just being here like this is fun enough for me. I don't need anything special."

He looked over at her. "A special girl deserves a special time."

Belle smiled. "You think so?"

"I know so."

Belle smiled inside for the rest of the way to Francine's house.

As soon as Belle saw Francine's big house and all the buggies parked out front, the butterflies in her stomach came back with a vengeance. How would Francine's friends treat her? Would they be accepting, or look down their noses? The last thing she wanted was to embarrass herself or Daniel, so she vowed not to do anything that might bring attention to herself while inside.

Their knock on the front door was met by a short, red-haired White man dressed in a very nice suit. He broke into a smile upon seeing Daniel. "Ah, Mr. Daniel, how are you?"

"Fine, Hodges. This is my cousin, Belle."

"Pleased to meet you, Miss Belle. May I take your cloak?"

Belle gave him the garment, all the while wondering where Hodges fit into Francine's family.

"Miss Franny's in the parlor," Hodges offered kindly. "Go on in."

After they left him, Belle quietly asked Daniel, "Is Hodges a member of the family?"

"Nope, he's the butler."

Belle's eyes widened. "She has a White servant?"

"Yep. It's not that uncommon."

It most certainly was where Belle came from. She'd never encountered such an arrangement before. "What does Francine's papa do?"

"He's in lumber."

The rest of Belle's questions had to be set aside because Francine pounced upon Daniel as soon as they entered the parlor.

"Hello, darling," she cooed, wrapping her arms around his waist. "You made it."

Francine was wearing a yellow gown with a sheer embroidered overdress that Belle knew some seamstress had sewn on for weeks.

Daniel smiled and gave his beautiful intended a quick peck on her forehead. "How are you?"

"Fine."

Francine then turned to Belle and seemed shocked by the way Belle looked in her finery. "Why, Belle. You look—"

Adam Morgan sidled up and filled in the blank, "Stunning?"

His brother Jeremiah slid to Belle's other side. "Spectacular?"

Belle couldn't help her grin. "How are you two?"

"Infinitely better now that you've arrived," Adam claimed.

His brother added, "The afternoon is much brighter. Come, let us introduce you around."

Each brother offered her an arm, so Belle played along and let them lead her away. For the next little while Belle was introduced to the ten or so other young people gathered for Francine's affair. She couldn't remember all of the names, but did notice that the young men seemed a lot more pleased to make her acquaintance than Francine's girlfriends did.

One girl, with a horse face and pale skin, critically looked Belle's gown up and down, then said, "I had a dress with a bodice similar to that, but it was so terribly out of fashion, I donated it to some poor runaway Francine's trying to help. Isn't she noble?"

Belle wondered how she was expected to respond to such a question.

Adam answered for her by cracking sarcastically, "Yes, Franny's so noble, we're thinking of taking up a collection and sending her to Liberia as a missionary."

That said, he led Belle away to an unoccupied chair on the far side of the room. Once she was seated she told him, "Thanks."

"It's what knights are for. If she offended you, just remember that everyone calls her Horse-Face Harriet, and that should make you feel better."

Belle smiled.

"That's my girl. How about some punch?"

"I'd love some."

So off he went, only to be replaced by his brother a second later. "Has Adam deserted you?"

"No, he went to get me some punch."

Belle knew good manners dictated she pay attention to Jeremiah, but her eyes kept straying across the room to Daniel standing so contentedly by Francine's side.

Jeremiah said, "They make a good-looking couple, don't they?"

Embarrassed that she'd been caught staring, Belle nodded. "Yes."

"Franny's a beautiful woman, but Dan deserves better. If he marries her, he'll want to hang himself within a week."

Belle looked over at him. "That's not nice to say."

"Ah, but it's the truth. Franny's beautiful to look at, but she's like a painting. All lacquer, no substance."

Adam returned with Belle's punch.

"Thank you," Belle told him as she took the crystal cup from his hand.

"You're welcome. What are you two gossiping about?"

"The beautiful but vapid Francine," Jeremiah confessed without shame.

Adam raised his cup. "One of my favorite subjects," he drawled sarcastically.

Belle shook her head with amusement. "You two need a keeper."

"We have one, but Francine's got him all tied up right now, so we're on our own."

"That's very frightening." Belle laughed.

Jeremiah replied, "You ain't seen nothing yet."

Daniel spent the afternoon listening to Francine go on about this and that, but his eyes were on Belle. He'd been watching her being escorted around by Adam and Jeremiah, and although he was grateful to them for taking her under their wings, he envied their time with her. He couldn't get over her transformation. The dress fit her well, and the ribbon circling her short hair gave her a playful but fetching air. Belle was truly lovely, but Daniel knew he was drawn to her by more than that. Francine detested going to rallies or listening to speeches, but he sensed Belle would not. Belle appreciated the gift of freedom. He seriously doubted Francine would have walked her feet raw for anything, unless it was a new hat. *Yet you're going to marry her,* his inner voice said. The questioning voice seemed to be growing stronger with each new day, but Daniel pushed it aside, and directed his full attention back to whatever Francine was talking about now.

As Francine went on and on about a new dress she'd seen in a Whittaker shop window, Daniel became distracted by the small group of people gathered around a card table. Excusing himself from Francine, he wandered over to see what was going on. To his surprise he found a seated Belle playing checkers. "Belle?" he asked questioningly.

She looked up, her eyes sparkling happily. "Hello, Daniel. Do you play?"

He nodded. "I do."

Jeremiah stepped up and pulled out the chair left vacant by Belle's last opponent. "Oh, do have a seat. She's beaten all comers so far."

Daniel wondered how many more fascinating facets his "cousin" Belle had hidden behind those coal-black eyes. Drawn by her, he sat, but warned, "I'm very good at this, Belle. They don't call me Best for nothing."

Everyone groaned at the awful pun, but Belle just smiled. "You can go first."

"No, ladies first."

And so it began.

Daniel had always been the reigning checker king of his set, able to trounce challengers in no time flat, but he soon realized that Belle was the checker *queen*. By the time the game wound down, Daniel had three men remaining; Belle had more kings than the Bible lined up on her side of the board.

In a kind voice she pointed out, "There's nothing you can do, Daniel. I have you."

Daniel continued to study the board as if looking for a way out of the traps she'd set. "Not until I concede, you don't." He looked up at her and grinned. "You're very good at this, Belle."

She grinned in response. Noticing the frowning Francine for the first time, Belle ignored her, then went back to studying the defeated Daniel. "Do you give?"

"No," he declared, then after a few more moments of study, said, "Yes, I give." He looked around and said, "Gentlemen, do not play checkers with this lady. Tell your friends."

He stood then, and the Morgan brothers began to applaud. Adam said, "Belle, you've no idea how happy you've made us. He's been whipping us mercilessly since he was ten."

Jere said, "Forget that; I think I'm in love. Marry me, Belle, and we could have lots of checker youngins."

Belle laughed, as did everyone else. Well, Francine didn't. Instead, she cracked, "Checkers. That quite a skill you have there, Belle. I thought slaves spent all their time picking cotton."

In the complete silence that followed, Belle heard a few muffled snickers. It was not a nice thing to say. Belle swore she'd pluck out her eyes if she started to cry, but she felt like she might.

Seeing Belle's face made Daniel's heart twist with pain. "Apologize, Francine."

Francine had the nerve to act offended. "Whatever for?"

"For being such a...it rhymes with witch!" Adam Morgan snapped.

"How dare you say that to me in my own house!"

An angry Jeremiah threw back, "You didn't care when it was Belle!"

"Get out!" Francine demanded.

Belle threw up her hands. "Stop this!"

You could hear a pin drop. Belle turned to Francine and said, "No, we slaves didn't spend all our time picking cotton. Any other nasty remarks?"

Belle's voice was so cutting, Francine shrank back.

Belle cracked, "Thought not."

The silence was thick enough to cut and serve on a plate. Belle turned her eyes on Daniel next, and she had to give it to him: he didn't flinch in the face of her quiet anger. She saw sympathy, but didn't expect him to take her side over his intended's.

Belle slowly scanned the rest of the young faces around the room. Some met her gaze with contempt and disdain, but a few had admiration in their eyes. Satisfied she now knew friends from those who would never be, Belle decided she'd endured enough for one afternoon. "Would you see me home?" she asked Jeremiah.

Both brothers stepped to her side, and Adam said quietly, "We'd be honored."

They offered her their arms. Without giving Daniel or Francine a backward glance, Belle let the Morgans escort her out.

Mrs. Best was in the parlor reading the paper when Belle returned. Cecilia took one look at Belle's distant face and set her paper aside. Standing, she asked with concern, "What's the matter? Where's Daniel?"

"He's still at Francine's."

Mrs. Best came closer. "How'd you get home?"

"The Morgans."

Mrs. Best peered into Belle's face. "Belle, did something happen?"

"I got into a row with Francine. Daniel will probably never speak to me again, but Mrs. Best, she's so mean."

Cecilia shook her head. "You didn't sock her, did you?"

Belle smiled. "No, but Lord knows I wanted to. Guess I'll never be invited back."

Mrs. Best smiled, too. "Probably not, but is that so bad?"

"No."

"Well, Francine was probably just jealous because you were the prettiest thing there. Go on up and change clothes. We can talk afterward, if you'd like."

"Thank you," Belle offered genuinely. "I'll see you later on."

Mrs. Best nodded.

Up in her room, Belle removed her dress and carefully hung it in the armoire. Off came Mrs. Best's borrowed hoop slips, the new slippers and the stockings that had been another surprise gift from Mrs. Best. Belle put on one of her old everyday dresses and tried to banish Francine's taunting remark from her mind. It was hard, though, and harder still to banish the image of Daniel's sympathetic eyes as he stood rooted to Francine's side. Belle had been having such a good time up until then; she'd actually thought she'd been accepted by Francine and Daniel's friends. *Silly me,* she said to herself. Had it not been for the Morgan brothers, she might still be there fielding Francine's verbal barbs.

Belle looked over at the basket holding the parts and pieces of the gown she was making for Mrs. Best. Bringing it over to the bed, Belle searched out her needles and went to work. No, she didn't pick cotton, but she could sew.

eleven

when Daniel returned later that evening, he found his parents and Jojo sitting and talking in the parlor. "Hello," he said.

"Hello," his mother replied, peering closely at his face. "What happened between Francine and Belle?"

Daniel's lips tightened. "Francine was particularly nasty. I tried to get her to apologize—"

Jojo interrupted. "But you couldn't, could you?"

Daniel's eyes were chilly. "No."

Mr. Best looked at Daniel with concern, and asked, "Are you sure she's the girl for you, son?"

"I know she isn't," Jojo interjected sarcastically.

Her mother cut her a look. "You are not in this conversation, Josephine."

Jojo replied grudgingly, "Yes, Mama."

Mrs. Best turned her attention back to her son. "Your father's question is a good one, Daniel. I promised myself I'd never interfere with my children's choice of a mate, and I've set aside my own feelings about Francine because you say you love her, but are you sure this is the person you want to spend the rest of your life with?"

Daniel didn't reply. No, he wasn't sure, hadn't been for

weeks now, but he was a man of his word, and he'd made a promise to Francine's mother.

His mother's next words brought him back. "Belle acted as if her feelings had been hurt badly."

He nodded. "They were. I should probably talk to her."

"Good, because she thinks you're never going to speak to her again. That must've been some row."

He shook his head at the memory. The hurt in Belle's eyes pained him still. "I'll tell you about it later. Is Belle in her room?"

"Yes."

"Then I'll be back in a few minutes."

Upstairs, Daniel softly knocked on the partially closed door.

Belle looked up from the gathering stitch she was running through one of the sleeves. "Come in."

Seeing Daniel made her go still for a moment, then, setting aside her sewing, she said, "Hello, Daniel."

He nodded a greeting. "Belle. Can we talk?"

"Sure."

"I—want to apologize—"

"You don't have to. Francine said it, not you."

Daniel held her eyes. He could still see the hurt lingering in them. "Francine had no right—"

"No, she didn't."

"Will you let me complete my sentences?"

Belle bit back a retort. "I'm sorry. Go ahead."

"Thank you," he replied, a bit exasperated. "What Francine said was wrong. I don't expect you to forgive her right away—"

Belle couldn't believe her ears. "But you want me to forgive her at some point. Is that what you're saying?"

"Well, yes. I don't want you two at odds—"

"Is she planning on apologizing?"

"Well, no—"

"Then, Daniel Best, what in the world are you thinking, hitching yourself to somebody like that?"

The words came out of Belle's mouth before she could call them back. "I'm sorry. That's not my place."

He shook his head. "No need to apologize. Truthfully, I've been asking myself the same question."

Belle stilled. "Really?" she asked softly.

He met her eyes and confessed, "Really, but—"

"But what?"

He shrugged. "Before her mother died two years ago, I promised her I'd take care of Franny."

"Do your folks know?"

"No, and please don't tell them. I have to work this out for myself."

Belle now understood. Daniel's sense of honor was at play here also. "You should talk to them. Your folks are very understanding; maybe they can help."

"But I made a promise, Belle."

"One you're coming to regret."

Daniel sighed with frustration. "That's the truth." And all he kept seeing was how crushed Belle looked after being cut down by Francine. "You'll keep my secret?"

"Yes."

"Thanks."

Their eyes held for a moment more.

Daniel said, "You're easy to talk to."

"Glad you think so. Does that make us friends?"

He nodded in response. "I think so."

They both smiled.

Belle asked, "So when do I get to whup you at checkers again, friend?"

"That was a fluke."

"Fluke, my foot. I can beat you with my eyes closed."

"You and me, downstairs for a rematch in, say, fifteen minutes?"

"You have a date, but it'll take me no time to send you packing."

"And I can't wait to make you eat those words."

Their grins filled the room.

Daniel said in parting, "Fifteen minutes."

Belle tossed back, "Don't forget your crying towel."

And so, the official friendship between Belle Palmer and Daniel Best began.

Downstairs, the checker game ended the same way the previous game had; only this time, Belle trounced him three games out of three.

Daniel finally pushed the board away and asked wondrously, "How do you do that?"

A triumphant Belle explained, "My mistress had a stable hand named Quincy. Quincy could play checkers like nobody's business and he and I would play every evening before I went to bed. It was one of the few amusements Mrs. Grayson allowed, so over the years I learned to play real well so Quincy wouldn't get fed up and find another partner."

Mr. Best patted her shoulder in admiration. "Never thought I'd see the day he'd get trounced three to nothing, but you, my dear, are a charmer. Keep whipping him. Humility's a good thing."

"Papa?!" Daniel laughed, his voice shot through with humorous disbelief.

Jojo asked Belle, "Do you think you can teach me to play that well? He's been beating me since the day I was born."

"Anytime, Jo," Belle offered. Belle looked across the table into Daniel's smile. "One more?" she asked.

Daniel looked back as if she were insane. "No." He chuckled. "I've left enough blood on the floor. Trounce Mama for a while."

Cecilia, seated across the parlor perusing the newspaper, shook her head. "Oh, no. I've no desire to be her next victim."

Belle looked around at the smiles on everyone's faces and noted once again how blessed she was to have been taken in by them. Even in the face of Francine's bitter remark, Belle felt loved and appreciated here. The only thing missing from her new life was her own parents. She continued to pray for a reunion with her father even though she knew the probability of it ever happening was becoming more remote with each passing day. At last report, neither Mr. Best nor any of the other conductors on his line had heard a word concerning his fate, but they promised to keep searching.

Daniel's soft voice broke into her thoughts. "Belle, are you all right?"

She nodded and smiled. "Yes. Just thinking how glad I am to be here."

Mr. Best offered up, "And we're glad to have you here. Anybody who can beat my boy at checkers can live here forever."

"Amen!" Jojo declared, and everyone laughed, even Daniel.

That evening as the Best household prepared for bed, Mrs. Best stuck her head around Belle's door. "Just came to check on you. It seems you and Daniel have sorted everything out."

Belle, dressed in her nightclothes, was in the process of turning back her sheets. "We did."

Mrs. Best looked pleased. "Good."

Mrs. Best came farther into the room, saying, "You know, I had to face a few Francines myself when I first came North."

"Did you?"

"Yes, though none of them were as fast, as mean or as spoiled as this Francine."

Belle raised an eyebrow. "Fast?"

"Fast," Mrs. Best repeated firmly.

Belle vowed to ask Jojo about that later.

Mrs. Best then asked pointedly, "Can you read, Belle?"

Belle dropped her eyes and slowly shook her head. "No, ma'am. And since I'm already sixteen, I figure I'm too old to learn. I don't really need reading to sew anyway."

"Mastering the written word is essential, Belle, no matter your age."

Belle searched her face. "You think so?"

"I know so. You can't best the Francines of the world without it."

Belle mulled that over for a moment. "Is learning how hard?"

"In some ways, yes. Other ways, no."

Belle thought on the idea some more. Did she really need to learn to read? Mrs. Best certainly seemed to think so. It was easy to see the benefits of an education; the members of the Best family were the smartest people she knew, but Belle wasn't sure book learning was for her. "Would I have to go to someplace and learn with little children?"

"No, dear. I'm sure we could work it out so you could be tutored here at home. No one wants you to be embarrassed in any way."

Belle found that encouraging. "Do I have to make a decision right now?"

Mrs. Best smiled kindly, "No. When you're ready just let someone know."

"All right."

The next day was Sunday, and Sunday meant church. During the first few weeks of Belle's stay with the Bests, she hadn't been allowed to attend services at the small, whitewashed African Methodist Episcopal church because of concerns for her safety. Slave catcher Otis Watson and his despicable, mounted minions were known to lurk in the trees surrounding the church before and after services. It was their way of sniffing out fresh prey. Since Belle was new to the community, the Bests didn't want her presence to pique his interest. Watson, however, seemed to have vanished; his livery had been closed for a fortnight, and no one had seen him, his men or his dogs.

As Mr. Best drove the wagon down the rutted road that led to the church, Mrs. Best sat beside him on the front seat. Behind them, on the bench in the wagon bed sat Daniel, Belle and Jojo. Everyone was dressed in their Sunday best. While the wagon rattled along, Belle noted the beauty of the glorious, blue-skied day. The trees had lost their early spring sparseness and were now full and leafy green. The wind was warm, and the lushness of the land stretched out as far as the eye could see. It was now the first week of May and Belle had been free a little over a month's time. Who knew this would be where life would lead her—Michigan, a place she'd never seen before, among people she'd never met. The only thing marring her complete contentment was the unknown fate of her father.

A short while later, Cecilia Best asked her husband, "Where do you think Watson could be?"

William shrugged his dark-suited shoulders. "Don't know. It's a question everybody's asking."

"Well," Cecilia said firmly, "if he shows up sniffing around our church today, I may shoot him myself."

Daniel laughed. "Mama, it's Sunday. You're not supposed to be talking about shooting people."

"I know, Lord forgive me, but we should be able to worship in peace. The sooner vermin like Watson are sent to stand before St. Peter, the better off we'll all be."

"Amen, Mama," Jojo chimed in supportively.

Belle grinned, but she, too wondered where Watson might be. She'd never met the man, nor did she have a desire to; anyone who made his living the way he did would not be considered a friend, but she knew the community would breathe easier if Watson's whereabouts were known.

The grove surrounding the church was filled with buggies and wagons. After Mr. Best parked the buggy, Daniel politely helped his sister step down and then it was Belle's turn. She had to force herself to remain calm as she placed her hand in his, and then pretend her heart wasn't beating like a drum when he guided her down.

"Thank you," she said softly when he turned her loose.

"You're welcome."

Still masking her reaction, Belle walked with him and his family toward the church.

As they approached, they were greeted enthusiastically by fellow parishioners. It was indeed a beautiful Sunday morning, and everyone in attendance seemed particularly pleased to see everyone else. Inside, the family found seats. While waiting for the service to begin, Belle and Jojo sat quietly but watched as people filed in. Jojo leaned over to her brother and whispered, "Franny's here."

Daniel turned and, like Belle, saw Francine being

escorted in by two men: one middle-aged and distinguished, the other young and handsome.

Because Belle had never seen either man before, she whispered into Jojo's ear, "Who's that she's with?"

Checking to make certain she wasn't going to draw her mama's ire for whispering in church, Jojo whispered back, "Her papa, and our teacher, Mr. Hood."

Belle wondered if Daniel noticed the proprietary hand the smiling, well-dressed Francine had on the handsome Mr. Hood's escorting arm. He must have, because Daniel watched them both a long time. When he turned back, his jaw was tight, his eyes directed straight ahead.

Before Belle had the chance to ask Jojo anything else, the pianist sounded the first rousing chords of the processional, and everyone stood.

Once the service was over, it was traditional for the members of the congregation to gather outside in the grove to drink punch, socialize and catch up on any news neighbors might have to share. Mr. Best was standing under one of the trees conferring in hushed tones with some of the men. Jojo had gone off to drink punch and giggle with her best friend Trudy Carr, leaving Belle to stand with Mrs. Best and Daniel.

Francine was making such a show of introducing Mr. Hood around, folks were beginning to look Daniel's way, as if gauging his reaction, but his face gave nothing away.

When Francine finally made her way over to where the Bests stood, she walked up with her hand still possessively holding on to Hood's arm, and said, "And these are the Bests. This is Mrs. Best, and her son, Daniel. This is Paul Hood."

Both Mrs. Best and Daniel nodded, but since Francine had made no mention of Belle, who stood right next to Daniel, Belle assumed she'd somehow been made invisible.

To let Mr. Hood know that she did exist, Belle said, "Hello, Mr. Hood. My name is Belle. I'm a Best cousin. Have you known Daniel's intended long?"

Hood stared first at Belle, then down at Francine. "Intended?!"

Daniel's smile was brittle. "Yes. Didn't Francine mention that?" Daniel noticed that Francine took that moment to fiddle with the bracelet on her arm and would not meet his eyes.

Hood, who appeared to be at least five years older than Daniel, looked Daniel up and down, then drawled, "Why, no. She hasn't. Pleased to meet you, Dan."

"Pleased, as well," Daniel allowed. The men shook hands grudgingly.

Francine playfully swatted Mr. Hood across the arm. "You teaser. I did tell you about Dani."

Hood responded by gazing down into her eyes, then declared, "Blame it on your beauty. It's rendered me so dim-witted, I must've forgotten."

Francine trilled a swoon, but Belle found the performance ridiculous.

Hood then turned to Daniel and said, "You've a fine lady here, Dan. Treat her well, or you'll have me to answer to."

Still avoiding Daniel's gaze, Francine gave a strained little laugh. "You are so silly. Come on. I see someone else I want you to meet."

With a wave to Daniel she was off.

Daniel seemed to have been turned to stone. Mrs. Best watched Francine's departure with a grimness in her eyes Belle had never seen before.

Mrs. Best told Belle, "Find Jojo. It's time to go. Daniel, you get the wagon; I'll get your father."

Belle hazarded a glance Daniel's way, then said, "Yes,

ma'am." Belle hurried off to fetch Jo. When she looked back Daniel was striding away.

An upset Daniel sat in the wagon. Was it his imagination, or did his intended show an uncommon interest in the new teacher? It was quite obvious Francine had been lying about having confessed to having a beau; Hood's surprise appeared genuine. Granted, Daniel could be wrong, and Francine's introducing Hood around could be totally innocent, but it didn't feel that way. Gut instinct told him something was going on between Francine and Paul Hood, and Daniel didn't know whether to applaud this surprising turn of events, or punch the teacher in the nose.

On the walk back to the wagon, Belle clued Jojo in on what had transpired. An angry Jo snapped, "She didn't tell Mr. Hood that she and Daniel are practically engaged?"

Belle shook her head. "Nope. His surprise looked real, Jo."

Jojo had nothing else to say, it seemed, because she and Belle crossed the rest of the church grove in silence.

When they reached the wagon, Mr. and Mrs. Best were already aboard, as was Daniel. He appeared to be staring off at a place only he could see. The appearance of Belle and his sister broke his reverie. He helped them both up to the wagon bed, then took his seat again. Not a word was said as Mr. Best turned the wagon's team back to the road.

A few miles from home, Mr. Best said to Belle, "Heard some real interesting news after church from one of the men today, Belle."

Her hopes rising, she asked, "About my father?"

"Yep, it seems one of Watson's friends down in Dayton, a man named Boyle, ran into problems escorting a bunch of fugitives back South."

"What kind of problems?"

"They escaped."

Belle's eyes widened.

Mr. Best added, "We're fairly sure your pa was one of those fugitives."

An excited Belle looked over at Jo and Daniel, who both met her eyes with smiles. Belle had so many questions she didn't know which one to ask first. "Did they get away?"

"Nine of the sixteen did."

Mrs. Best, looking surprised, asked, "When was this, William?"

"About two weeks ago. Since then, every slave-catching gang from here to the Kentucky border has been hunting them."

Daniel asked then, "Do you think Watson's riding with them, and that's why we've not seen him around?"

His father nodded. "Possibly. Seems this man Boyle is a fairly new trafficker, and his farm serves as a pen for folks being funneled back South."

"So," Belle said, "Watson and his cronies take all their captives to Dayton and this man handles the captives from that point?"

"Yes."

"But how can anyone be sure my pa was one of the nine?"

"He and a few of the nine made it to a station near Columbus. Last night, one of our committee members returned from visiting his sister there. She's a conductor, too, and your pa is hiding at her house. Or at least was; they've probably moved him by now."

Belle was speechless. He was safe? "But how did he know it was my pa?"

"Your father asked about you."

Belle went silent, then tears slowly filled her eyes. "He asked about me?"

Jojo put a comforting arm around Belle's shoulders and gave them a comforting quick squeeze.

Mr. Best nodded. "Yes, when our friend and his sister questioned the runaways about having family anywhere near, your pa told the story of being separated from you. Our friend knew of your plight because your case has been a priority for us here in Whittaker."

Belle asked, "Did your friend tell Pa I was here safe?"

"Yes, he did."

The happy tears ran down her face and she dashed them away with the backs of her hands. "Why couldn't my father just come back with your friend?"

"Too dangerous. Catchers are everywhere: on the roads, watching train depots. They're even raiding some of our stations. They want your pa and the others found and found quickly. Slave owners don't pay if the slaves aren't returned. Losing nine of them certainly won't enhance this Boyle's reputation."

"So when do you think I'll be able to see him?"

Mr. Best shrugged as he drove. "Truthfully? We don't know. As I've said, he's probably been moved elsewhere by now. Our friend's sister promises to keep us aware of his transfer soon. Much depends on the slave catchers. If they give up and go after other souls, you may see your father before too long, but if Watson and the others take it upon themselves to keep looking for as long as it takes, it could be winter."

Mrs. Best turned around so she could see Belle. "It really is wonderful news, Belle."

"I know, Mrs. Best, but I want to see him now, this moment."

Mrs. Best smiled understandingly. "You will. It might not be at this moment, but you will."

An elated Belle sank back against the seat. *My papa's alive!* And that was all she could think about for the rest of the ride home.

twelve

After church Daniel spent the afternoon brooding alone in his room. He was happy that Belle finally had received news of her father, but Daniel kept seeing Francine and Paul Hood. Coming to a decision, he left his room to seek out his parents.

They were out back, on the swing. Many years ago, when Daniel was small, William Best built Cecilia a big, pew-length porch swing and suspended it behind the house from the thick branches of one of the oldest and shadiest elms on the property. The swing was taken down every November, but put back up every May so that the two of them could enjoy the cool evening breeze at the end of the day. One evening when Daniel and Jo were much younger, they'd caught their parents sharing a kiss out here, and he remembered how terribly embarrassed he and his sister had been. As Daniel walked up now, they were just relaxing on a fine Sunday afternoon.

"I think I'm going to ride over to Francine's, if that's okay," Daniel said to them.

His mother, seated next to his father, nodded. "That's fine, son. I'll save you some supper, if you're not back."

With sudden insight, William said, "If it's worth anything, we'll support whatever decision you make concerning Francine and your future."

The words of confidence made Daniel feel good inside. "It's worth a great deal. Thanks, Pa. I'll be back later."

Bolstered by his parents' blessings, Daniel saddled up his horse. He had a few questions he wanted to ask Francine and he intended to get some answers. When he got to her house, however, she wasn't home.

Hodges met Daniel at the door. "Francine and her father have taken Mr. Hood to dinner at a friend's home. I'll let her know you stopped by."

Tight-lipped, Daniel said, "Thanks, Hodges."

"Good-bye, Mr. Daniel."

Moments later, Daniel and his horse were heading home. Out of all fairness, Daniel knew he had to hear Francine's side of the story before any final decisions could be made, but it certainly felt like the beginning of the end to him.

Very late that night, sounds of someone pounding forcefully on the front door awakened the entire Best household. In bed, Belle struggled to sit up. She had just shaken off the sleep well enough to open her eyes when Mrs. Best hastened into her room.

"Get up, Belle. Slave catchers are downstairs. They're looking for Nelson Parker."

Belle's eyes widened. "The man in the crate?"

"Yes. Grab a robe and come downstairs. Don't say a word unless you're spoken to directly. Hurry, dear; I'm going to wake Jo."

Mrs. Best must have sensed Belle's fear because she stopped and looked back, saying, "It'll be all right. We've had them here before. They won't find out anything, especially not about you."

Belle was still scared but hurried to put on her robe.

Downstairs she nervously entered the parlor to join the rest of the family. As she went to stand beside Jojo and her mama, Belle saw that already in the room were, along with Daniel and his father, Sheriff Lawson and another White man wearing a battered, sweat-soiled hat and a long, threadbare coat. He was as tall and thin as a scarecrow and had a hollow, ghoulish face to match. Belle had no idea who he might be, but he was by far the dirtiest, smelliest man of any race she'd ever encountered. His unwashed body filled the air with the thick, foul scent of dogs, horses and sweat.

The man had surveyed Belle closely when she entered, and now asked, "Who's she?"

Belle looked away from his blackened gums and yellow, stunted teeth.

Mr. Best answered, "My wife's niece, Belle."

"She's free, too, I suppose?" the man tossed back sarcastically.

"Yes, she is," William Best responded coolly. "The sheriff has her papers on file."

Jojo reached out and took Belle's hand. Jojo's cold hand was shaking. Belle squeezed it reassuringly. She looked over at Daniel. His eyes were angry, his face tight.

The man looked Belle up and down for a fright-filled moment more. "You know," he drawled malevolently, "I can smell runaways a mile away and this place stinks with them."

When he turned away from Belle, she willed her heart to stop racing, then wondered if his nose was so keen why couldn't he smell himself?

From the conversations that followed, Belle learned that

the man was Otis Watson. It gave Belle a modicum of relief to know Watson was here and not out hunting her father.

His voice refocused her attention. "I'm also looking for some nigras that ran away from a friend of mine down in Ohio. You people know anything about that?"

When no one confessed, Watson declared, "Well, that's a good thing because I got six mounted men and a passel of hunting hounds stationed outside. My hounds are real partial to dark meat—if you catch my meaning," he added with a malevolent, black-gummed grin.

Mr. Best stiffened in response to the bigoted taunt, but remained silent.

Watson spent a few more moments looking them all over before saying, "Now, back to this Parker. We know he was shipped to Pennsylvania and then on to here because the White man who crated him confessed, just before they put his abolitionist arse in the Richmond jail last week. He's gonna serve eight years for aiding your kind."

He cackled like a demon. Belle fought to keep her shudders from being seen.

William Best responded brittlely, "Well, we've no knowledge of this Parker or his whereabouts."

"Maybe not now, but you were involved. I know it," Watson accused.

"You're wrong."

It was a standoff.

Sheriff Lawson seemed to be as tired of Watson as the Bests and Belle were because the lawman asked tightly, "Is there anything else you want here, Watson? These nice folks would like to go back to sleep."

Otis Watson snarled a scarecrow smile. "Yeah, I want to search the house."

By law, the Bests had no right to prohibit a slave catcher with a federal warrant from searching the house. Belle had been told by Jojo that as a warning to other abolitionists, catchers were known to leave homes in shambles after a search. Belle prayed the Bests wouldn't be subjected to such treatment.

For the next hour, Watson and two of his men left their muddy boot prints all over Mrs. Best's newly mopped floors, and their foul scent in every room. They searched the kitchen, the cellar and under beds. They opened cupboards, looked up the flue, and threw back the rugs in a hunt for trapdoors. They even searched the barn where Mr. Best and Daniel worked. Belle knew they hoped to find some evidence of Nelson Parker's crate, but it had been reduced to kindling only a few hours after Mr. and Mrs. Best's return home that day.

The catchers found nothing. When they wanted to bring in the dogs, Sheriff Lawson put his foot down. "You've searched once. The act doesn't give you the right to search again and again, so we are done here. Good night, Mr. and Mrs. Best; my apologies for all this."

Watson puffed up like an adder. "But—"

The sheriff warned firmly, "Say good night, Mr. Watson."

Instead, Watson turned to William Best. "One day, Best. One day."

Ignoring him, Mr. Best said, "Good night, Sheriff, and no apologies needed. We know you're just doing your job, as distasteful as it may be."

Sheriff Lawson smiled wanly. "Thanks." He then told Watson and his companion, "Let's go."

Once Watson was gone, the fuming Cecilia Best declared, "Open every window in the house. I refuse to sleep with that man's stench in my nostrils. Keen nose, my foot. Can he smell soap and water?!"

Everybody chuckled. The tension was broken. Cecilia marched back up to her room. The rest of the family gladly opened the windows, then went back to their beds.

Very early the next morning, a frantic Bea Meldrum arrived at the Bests' front door bearing terrible news. "Watson's got the Morgan boys."

Belle, standing with the Bests in the doorway, felt her stomach sicken.

Cecilia Best whispered, "Dear Lord."

"When?" Mr. Best demanded.

"Last night, real late. No warrant, no trial. He just took them."

"Must've been after they were here," Mr. Best said angrily.

Daniel asked his father, "Do you think Adam and Jere may have said something about delivering the crate?"

His father shrugged. "Who knows? Watson doesn't need an excuse. Maybe he's trying to replace those slaves that escaped in Ohio. Did anybody notify the sheriff, Bea?"

Bea nodded. "Yes, but he says there's nothing he can do. Watson's got a good four hours' start on him. Those boys could be anywhere."

Cecilia asked, "What about their mother, did they take her, too?"

"She's unharmed, but was left behind, tied up. She's heartbroken, of course."

Belle couldn't believe her ears. She saw that Jojo had tears in her eyes.

Bea's voice was grim. "The Vigilance Committee's going to meet soon as everyone can get to the church. I'll see you and Dani there."

She left to further spread the tragic news. William and Daniel hurried off to change out of their nightclothes and head over to the meeting.

Belle didn't understand how this could happen. "But aren't Adam and Jeremiah free?"

Cecilia nodded. "Yes, but the act doesn't care."

"Isn't there something we can do?"

"Pray that the committee can find them and somehow bring them home."

Cecilia walked over and pulled her teary-eyed daughter into her arms. Jojo held on to her mother tightly, then whispered sadly, "Oh, Mama, why can't they just leave us alone?"

Mrs. Best leaned down and kissed Jojo's brown forehead. "Don't cry, sweetling. We'll find them, and one day soon slave catchers will be a thing of the past."

But when? Belle wondered angrily. *When?*

After the Morgans' kidnapping, a tense watchfulness spread over the community. In addition to Jeremiah and Adam, six other people were taken South by Watson: two men, a woman and a father and his two young sons. The Vigilance Committee met until late that evening, and according to the report Daniel and Mr. Best gave the family upon their return home, every conductor on the line, from Michigan southward had been alerted to keep an eye out. With any luck, Watson would be waylaid and his victims rescued, but no one knew if more kidnappings would follow, so women were instructed to hang out the quilts that signaled the area temporarily unsafe for fugitives, and the freedom lamps of the miniature jockeys were extinguished all over the county. People stayed close to home, and at night, the men sat with shotguns at the ready in case they needed to defend their families.

On Saturday, Belle and the Bests piled into the wagon and made the drive to Detroit for a rally at Second Baptist Church. The rally had been scheduled many months ago, but now with the kidnappings fresh in everyone's mind, many more people planned to attend.

It was Belle's first opportunity to see the area's abolitionists gathered en masse, and it was impressive. Almost two hundred folks of all races and genders had traveled to the church from as far away as Dayton, Ohio, and Amherstburg, Ontario, to attend. They came bearing banners that decried slavery, and offering donations to the committee to help with the search for the Morgans and the others. Representing Detroit's all-Black committee were the famous William Lambert and George DeBaptiste. The Detroit group, also known as the Order of the African Mysteries, had transported thousands of runaways to freedom and, according to Mrs. Best, were one of the most secretive abolitionist organizations in the country. Their coded communications and cryptic doings had become the model for vigilance communities everywhere. Both Lambert and DeBaptiste spoke eloquently and forcefully. In addition to denouncing slavery and those who profited from it, they urged the gathered crowd to arm themselves against the slave catchers, so as to meet force with force when necessary, as the good citizens of Christiana, Pennsylvania, had done in 1851. DeBaptiste then quoted Daniel's idol, the great Frederick Douglass, by saying the only good slave catcher was a dead one. When he concluded, his rousing remarks were met with enthusiastic shouts and applause from the crowd.

Daniel leaned over and told the wildly applauding Belle that slave owners in Kentucky had put a thousand-dollar bounty on DeBaptiste's head for his role in aiding fugitives, but so far, no one had been bold enough or stupid enough to try and collect.

After the main speakers were finished, the pulpit was turned over to lesser-known individuals, and to Belle's surprise and delight, Daniel and his mother were among them. Mrs. Best issued a rousing call to the women gathered to increase their efforts in aiding abolition. She cited the activities of females all over the North who were agitating, raising funds and forming societies in the name of freedom. Daniel delivered an impassioned plea on why slavery needed to die and then spoke from the heart about the kidnappings of his two best friends. Belle was so very proud and thought him the handsomest young man in the church.

The speakers were followed by a mass choir, whose singing filled both the church and the hearts of those in attendance with their message of perseverance and faith. At the end of the day, over one hundred dollars had been raised, and Belle went home with the Bests determined to do all she could to help aid the cause.

"The Morgan boys have been found!" Mrs. Best declared excitedly as she escorted a smiling Bea Meldrum into the house. It was now the end of May, and it had been more than three weeks since the kidnapping.

Mrs. Best's ecstatic voice brought everyone hurrying into the parlor.

Bea told them all, "An attorney friend of Mr. Still's in Philadelphia found them in Richmond, Virginia. I just left their mother. She showed me the letter she received from him yesterday."

"Hallelujah!" William Best shouted happily.

Belle looked to Daniel and they shared a grin. He'd taken the kidnapping of his friends very hard.

A happy Jojo asked, "What else did the attorney write, Mrs. Meldrum?"

"Well, it seems Watson sold the brothers to a Kentucky trader who took them by train to the slave pens in Richmond. They were then sold at a public auction for twenty-six hundred dollars."

Daniel whistled appreciatively. "Who knew those two woodenheads would be worth so much?"

His mother cut him a look. "This is serious, Daniel."

"I know, Mama. Sorry."

She peered over at him and said, "But you are right."

Everyone allowed themselves a small smile.

Belle asked then, "So, where are they now? Are they on their way back here?"

"No," Bea said. "They're awaiting a hearing before a local judge. This auction took place two days before the attorney found them, but luckily the bidder hadn't paid yet. Once the attorney can prove the boys are who they say they are, their mother expects they'll be declared free and sent home."

Belle felt relief take hold.

Daniel asked, "How long might that be?"

"A week or two, three at the most, she thinks." Bea added, "The letter was mailed from Richmond six days ago, so hopefully everything's being worked out."

Mr. Best added sagely, "Those boys are lucky. They could've disappeared into the South and never been heard from again."

Belle knew he was right. After all, hadn't she lost her mother and almost her father? She was glad the Morgans were coming home, though. She liked them both and would continue to pray for their quick and safe return.

Even though it appeared as if Adam and Jere would be

freed, the vigilance in the community continued. Some of Watson's lieutenants were still roaming around, and folks stayed on alert. The number of runaways entering the area had been reduced to a trickle, and any freight that had to be moved was done under very tight security.

One evening, a few days after the Morgan news, Belle asked Mrs. Best if she would come up to her room for a moment. Mrs. Best appeared a bit puzzled by Belle's mysterious request, but she set aside her household accounts and followed Belle back upstairs.

Upon entering the room, Belle said, "Have a seat on the bed here, and close your eyes."

Mrs. Best looked first to Belle and then to her seated and grinning daughter. "What is this about?" she asked.

Jojo implored, "Just close your eyes, Mama. It's a surprise."

"All right, no shenanigans now," Mrs. Best warned, then covered her eyes.

Once the girls were certain she wasn't peeking, they prepared everything, then Belle declared, "You may open them."

The burgundy gown was finished. When Mrs. Best saw it in all its beautiful glory she brought her hands to her mouth in wonder. "Oh, Belle, it's gorgeous." Mrs. Best slowly came off the bed and walked over to where Belle stood holding up the gown. All she seemed able to say was, "My goodness, Belle."

Jojo said, "You're going to have the prettiest dress in the whole place."

The overskirt had been lavishly embroidered, and the jet lace trim added just the right touch. The high-necked bodice with its gauzy jet inset didn't have a pucker or a seam out of place. When she wore the dress over the requisite hooped slips, Mrs. Best would be able to glide through the ball like a queen.

Belle enjoyed the pleasure on Mrs. Best's face almost as much as she'd enjoyed making the gown. Belle considered all her hard work just a small payment on the enormous debt she owed Cecilia Best and her family. "How about you get your fancy shoes and we hem it up?"

Mrs. Best didn't have to be asked twice. She was gone and back in a flash.

After the dress was hemmed, it was wrapped in tissue paper, and then hung in Mrs. Best's armoire. The ball was next weekend and Belle and Jojo couldn't wait to see her all fancied up.

Back in Belle's room, Jojo helped Belle put her sewing items back into her basket. "Papa's eyes are going to pop right out of his head when he sees Mama in that dress," she told Belle. "She's never worn anything that beautiful before."

"Well, she deserves it."

Josephine met Belle's eyes, and she said genuinely, "You made her real happy, Belle. Thank you."

Belle felt her heart swell. "You're real welcome, Jo."

"When I get married, will you make my dress?"

"Certainly, but that's not going to be anytime soon, is it?" Belle teased, sifting through her threads to see what she had left over.

Jo, now posed before the mirror, said, "No." She then began lifting her heavy brown sausage curls this way and that. "I'm thinking about cutting my hair."

"I hope your trunks are packed, because you'll need someplace to live once your mama gets done with you."

Jojo sighed. "I know, but I'm just so tired of looking twelve."

Belle chuckled. "You are twelve, Jojo."

"And I'll probably stay this way forever. Sausage curls and petticoats," she said dejectedly. "I look like the Medusa."

"Who's the Medusa?"

"A woman from Greek mythology. She had snakes for hair."

"Excuse me?"

Jo turned from the mirror. "Yep, and if you looked her in the face, you'd be turned into stone."

Belle stared. "Really?"

"Truly. We're studying the Greek myths, and the stories are filled with all manner of strange folks. Centaurs, gods, muses."

Belle had no idea what a centaur or a muse was, but found the names curious. "Are they supposed to have been real people?"

Jojo shrugged. "Mr. Hood says no, but he didn't seem real certain."

Belle couldn't see a snake-haired woman being real, but knew there were probably thousands of things she had no knowledge of. "How's your handsome Mr. Hood doing, by the way? Are all the girls still swooning?"

"No."

The answer was such an abrupt one, Belle studied Jojo silently. "What's happened?"

Jojo didn't answer for a moment. She then met Belle's eyes with such a serious face, Belle couldn't imagine what had come over her young friend. "Jo, whatever's wrong?" It was obvious Jojo was wrestling with something, so Belle waited for her to speak.

When she did, she began in a small voice, "Belle, if you know something that you know will hurt somebody you love, do you tell them anyway?"

Belle searched Jojo's honest eyes. "I don't know, Jo. Depends on what it is, I suppose. Is this something you need to talk to your mama about?"

Jo shook her head. "I'd like to, but I can't. She'd have a fit."

Belle couldn't imagine what this concerned, but searched her mind for a trusted adult Jojo might consult. "How about Mrs. Meldrum? She seems real nice."

"She'd just tell Mama."

"Your brother?"

Jo's eyes widened. "Heavens no!"

"Okay," Belle said, noting Jo's strong reaction. "What about your friend, Trudy?"

"Trudy knows already."

Jo then looked to Belle, and Belle knew what was next. Even though Belle wasn't sure she wanted to be Jojo's confidante in this, she refused to turn her back on the girl who'd brought such joy into her life. "Do you wish to tell me?"

Jo scanned Belle's face. "Are you sure?"

Belle nodded. "Sounds like it's a burden that needs to be shared, so yes, I'm sure."

"Francine's been sparking with Mr. Hood."

Belle froze. She stared. She said, "What?!"

Jojo nodded unhappily. "They eat lunch together almost every day, now that we're meeting in the church basement for school."

Belle now understood why Jojo needed to talk this over. "Does Francine know that you know?"

She shrugged. "I don't think she cares, frankly. You see, she came by Trudy's house when we were having school there last month."

"What did she want?"

"Oh, she brought some books her papa had purchased

for Mr. Hood, but she didn't leave. She spent the whole day swooning just like us. She's been bringing him lunch at least three times a week since then."

"Maybe she's just being kind. The man doesn't have any family here, right?"

"Right, but this is Francine the Queen we're discussing here—she doesn't know anything about being kind."

Belle had to admit, Jojo did have a point. "It certainly sounds suspicious, Jo, especially after that show she made in church a few Sundays back, but if they're only eating lunch—"

"And kissing."

"Kissing?" Bell croaked.

Jojo nodded like a horse. "Kissing."

Belle's hands went to her mouth. Daniel would be devastated. "Jo, this is terrible."

"I know. I'm having trouble sleeping because I don't know if I should tell Daniel or not."

Belle understood. How do you tell your brother that the woman he plans to marry is courting with someone else? In light of the secret Daniel had shared about his promise to Francine's mother, Belle found this to be good news in a way; it would give Daniel an out if he chose to take it, but if he was truly intent upon making Francine his bride, it would break his heart.

Jo asked, "So what do we do? Do we tell him?"

Belle hadn't a clue as to how to proceed. She shrugged. "I don't know."

The two of them shared a look, then Jo said, "Well, at least I feel better having told someone else."

Belle, not sure how she felt, cracked, "Thanks a lot."

Jojo smiled.

Belle had come to a decision. "Well, let's not tell Daniel for now. Maybe something will happen, and he'll find out on his own."

"I hope so, because if Mama finds out first, she'll turn Francine into stone for sure."

Belle didn't doubt that for a moment.

thirteen

Late Saturday afternoon, Belle and Jojo helped Mrs. Best prepare for the ball. Jojo did her mother's hair, then both girls stood by as she donned the dress. Belle surveyed her handiwork with a critical eye: looking at the fit, how the seams appeared, whether she'd inserted the tops of the sleeves smoothly enough. She ran her eyes down the lines of the waist, searching for puckers or anything that was not right, but she found no flaws in her work. It was the first gown she'd ever made for a loved one, and it showed.

Mrs. Best gazed at herself in the mirror, then spent a few smiling moments turning back and forth to see the gown from all angles. "Belle, I don't know how to thank you. Once the word gets around about your skills, the ladies will be lined up at our door."

Belle was glad to see Cecilia Best so happy. "Maybe then I can start paying you some room and board."

Cecilia stilled, turned, and gave Belle a long, penetrating look. "Young lady, be glad I'm all gussied up, otherwise you and I would go toe to toe over that remark. Room and board. I should be paying you for all the work you do around here." Cecilia then told Jojo, "Smack her for me, would you, Jo? I don't want to muss anything."

The three women all grinned.

* * *

Belle and Jojo made sure Daniel and Mr. Best were waiting at the foot of the stairs before they would let Mrs. Best make her appearance. Once everyone was in place, Jojo declared in a loud voice, "Presenting Mrs. Cecilia Best."

Mrs. Best came forward. Her men took one look at her standing on the landing and their chins dropped. In her beautiful burgundy silk with her hair done up and just a touch of paint on her face, she descended the stairs slowly. Mr. Best had such a look of wonder on his face, Belle couldn't hold her grin.

Mr. Best finally found speech, it seemed. "Lord, Cecilia. You're even more beautiful than the day we married."

She told him softly, "Do I know you?"

He grinned and played right along. "No. Let me introduce myself. My name is William Best."

"Pleased to meet you, William Best. Is your carriage ready?"

He nodded. "Oh, yes, my dear. Very ready."

Amused, Belle tried not to stare. She'd never known married people flirted this way until she came to live here. On one hand, watching their antics sometimes made Belle very embarrassed, but on the other hand, she hoped to have such an easygoing relationship with the man she married someday. Belle looked to Daniel to gauge his reaction and found him watching her so seriously and so intently, her knees went weak.

Mrs. Best's voice distracted her. "Jo, in bed at a decent hour. I know tomorrow's Sunday, but you will be going to church. Belle and Daniel, not too late, and keep an eye out. Watson's heathens are still around."

They both nodded.

She then turned back to her husband who was still

staring at her as if she were dessert. She smiled up at him and said sweetly, "Are you ready, William?"

He nodded, then told his son, "If you're still awake when your mother and I get home, do not disturb us unless the house is on fire. Do you understand?"

Daniel tried to hide his grin, but failed. "Yes, sir. Have a good time."

"Oh, we will," his father assured him, still eyeing his lovely wife. "Don't you worry about that."

And then they were gone.

In the silence that followed, Jojo said, "They're really too old to be acting that way. I'm glad none of my friends were here."

Belle chuckled. "I think they're sweet. Do they embarrass you, too, Daniel?"

Daniel told her, "No. I plan to love the woman I marry just as much as Papa loves Mama."

His eyes were once again holding Belle's with such intensity, she found it a bit hard to breathe. Why would he say such a thing to her? Was it because they'd decided to be friends, and he was just being truthful in response to that friendship, or was it about something else entirely? Belle had no answers, but knew her crush on him would never go away if he kept looking at her like that. She nervously turned her eyes back to Jojo, and found Jojo watching them. Jo had that knowing little smile on her face again. Belle asked, "Yes?"

Jojo just shook her head. "Nothing. I'll see you two later. I have some schoolwork to do. Let me know when it's time to cut the cake."

The cake, made by Belle this morning, was for dessert, along with the ice cream hardening in the churn.

Jojo disappeared up the stairs.

In the silent aftermath, Belle could feel uncertainty rising within her again. Her desire to retreat to her room warred with wanting to stay and be with Daniel.

Daniel wanted Belle to sit and talk with him awhile, but didn't know if he should ask her. He decided he would. "Are you going up to your room?"

"I—maybe, I hadn't decided."

"Will you sit and talk with me for a while? That is, if you want to."

Belle willed herself to respond calmly. "I'd like that."

Daniel gestured her to a seat on the settee, then he sat down at her side.

An awkward silence rose between them. Belle searched her mind for something to say or to discuss. "What did you want to be when you were younger?"

"Older," he cracked with a smile, then said, "Really, I wanted to be a carpenter, just like my father. I would watch him take pieces of wood and turn them into polished tables and drawers and beds, and I wanted to do those things, too. What did you want to be?"

"I don't remember ever wanting to be anything," she answered truthfully, "maybe because I knew that I'd always be just what I was. I always dreamed of doing things, though."

"Such as?"

"Seeing all the fancy balls my dresses and gowns were being worn to. Going on some of the sea voyages and trips the young ladies took those same gowns on. The things I sewed got to see more of the world than I ever did. Until I came here."

Belle held his eyes. She wondered what it would be like to see the world with him.

Daniel now understood what poets meant about

drowning in a woman's eyes. "What did you do before you learned to sew?"

"Helped Mama keep Mrs. Grayson's house. She was Mrs. Grayson's housekeeper, but she was a seamstress, too, much better than I'll ever be probably."

"Well, the dress you made was beautiful. Mama looked grand."

"Thank you, Daniel, and yes, she did."

"And you promised me a shirt, remember?"

"I know, I haven't forgotten."

Daniel sensed he was with the shy, unsure Belle this evening, although he knew the sassy-talking, checker-playing parts of her weren't far away. He enjoyed both versions of her, however. "I'd ask if you'd like to play checkers, but you'll only trounce me again, so no sense in that."

Belle lowered her head to hide her smile. "It would be fun, though."

"Trouncing me?" he asked with an amazed look on his handsome face.

"Yes."

"No." He laughed. "Think of something else."

"We could cut the cake," Belle offered in conspiratorial tones.

Daniel smiled again. "A woman after my own heart."

Those words made their eyes meet and hold. As if governed by a mind of its own, Daniel's hand reached out and the fingers slowly traced Belle's smooth, dark cheek. Belle, trembling like a leaf in the wind, closed her eyes as he leaned over and touched his lips to hers, first once and then twice, the second time deeper, softer. It was her very first kiss and it was everything she'd ever dreamed it would be.

Her eyes were still closed when he slowly eased away. Shimmering like sunlight on newly fallen snow, Belle rode the wave of the new and wonderful sensations, then slowly opened her eyes.

Daniel didn't know whether to apologize or kiss her again. Honor won out. "I'm sorry, I probably shouldn't've done that."

Belle met his gaze hesitantly. "No apology needed. It was rather nice."

He smiled. "You think so?"

"I've nothing to compare it with, but yes."

For some reason Daniel was glad to know she'd never been kissed before. "Guess this sort of complicates that friendship we talked of having."

"It complicates many things," she replied quietly. Belle wanted to be his sweetheart and his friend, but one of those roles was already held by Francine. Belle came to a very painful decision. "I can't let you kiss me again, Daniel. I know there are girls who wouldn't mind you having an intended, but I'm not one."

Daniel's lips thinned. "I know, Belle, and I understand." Daniel really did; he also understood that he had some thinking and deciding to do, but Lord, he wanted to hold her and kiss her until the cows came home. "Maybe we should see about that cake."

"Good idea."

They went into the kitchen, both as aware of each other as of their own heartbeats. Belle took down the bowls and he went to the back porch for the churn. Belle took a moment to call Jojo. When Belle returned to the kitchen, Daniel was just bringing in the churn, and once again, Belle thought him the finest young man the good Lord ever made. The kiss he'd given her continued to echo, making her want just one more.

Daniel could see the interest in her eyes and it resparked his own. "Stop looking at me that way, Belle."

She asked innocently, "What way?"

"Like you want to be kissed again."

"That wasn't what I was thinking, Mr. Swelled Head."

"Stop lying," he teased back, and bent to take the top off the ice cream. "I could see it in your eyes."

Jojo came in on the heels of that remark, asking, "You could see what in her eyes?"

Her brother cracked, "That you are a pest, pest."

Jojo stuck out her tongue.

They took their desserts into the parlor and sat at the dining table. Belle was positioned directly across from Daniel. Every time she looked up, his eyes were there, watching, studying, flirting.

She wanted to tell him to stop it, but didn't want Jo to know what was going on; things were complicated enough.

Jojo ate a bite of the cake and hummed with pleasure. "I love burnt-sugar icing. I'm glad you made this, Belle."

"Me, too," Daniel echoed.

Belle looked at him from beneath her lashes. "You're welcome."

Later, as Belle undressed for bed in the silence of her room, she let her mind replay Daniel's kiss. The bright, sparkling feelings returned, bringing with them the happiness she'd felt, and the wish that it might happen again. She set the wish aside though; his kisses were reserved for Francine; she was the one he planned to marry.

At that moment, Belle envied Francine more than anything. To be able to spend the rest of her life at Daniel's side would be a dream come true, but it would remain that, just a dream. No man in his right mind would toss Francine over for an illiterate runaway whose only talent was sewing, and Belle had more respect for herself than to enter into a relationship that led nowhere. No, she had the memories of their kiss, and she'd have to be content with that, because in reality, there couldn't be more.

Down the hall, Daniel lay in bed looking up at his ceiling. His room was as dark as the rest of the house, but he couldn't sleep. He had no idea what to do. Now that he'd kissed Belle, he wanted to be able to pursue her, court her, but Francine was in the way. Thinking of Francine as an impediment wasn't something he'd admitted to himself before. When had he changed? He knew the answer: the moment he met Belle. He remembered mistaking her for a boy at first, only to find out she was a whole lot more girl than he'd first believed possible. She'd really enjoyed the rally in Detroit, something Francine had never done when she'd gone with him. With Francine, it was always too many people, or the weather wasn't perfect, or she had nothing to wear. But Belle had gotten into the spirit of the event; she'd enjoyed the speakers, asked questions about some of the people on the dais and heartily applauded when he finished his speech. Belle was the kind of woman a man would be proud to court and make his wife. In many ways, she reminded him of his mother. When Belle married, he knew instinctively that she would be a helpmate, a supporter of her husband's life, not spend time trying to drag him to dinner parties, or fussing because he preferred working for the Cause to shopping in Windsor.

Daniel ran his hands over his eyes. This was a mess; a full-blown, hog-wild mess. And he hadn't a clue as to what to do.

In response to a note delivered by Bea a few days later from Mrs. Morgan, the entire Best clan, Belle included, drove to Ann Arbor to meet the train that would be bringing Adam and Jeremiah Morgan home. Mrs. Morgan, a woman who bore a strong resemblance to her two curly-haired sons, was already at trackside. Upon seeing the Bests, she gave Cecilia and William grateful hugs of thanks, saying to Mr. Best, "William, if you and the committee hadn't contacted Mr. Still and his friends in Philadelphia so swiftly, I might have lost my boys forever. Thank you."

"You're welcome," he returned emotionally.

Mrs. Morgan greeted Daniel and Jojo, too, then Daniel introduced her to Belle.

Mrs. Morgan smiled. "Belle, it's nice to meet you. My sons were right; you are very *belle*."

Embarrassment burned Belle's cheeks. She didn't consider herself beautiful at all, and wondered why the Morgans kept saying that.

But everything was set aside as the train pulled into the station in a hail of noise, cinder and soot. Everyone jumped back to avoid the ash and embers pouring from the stack, but also kept an eye peeled for Jeremiah and Adam.

Jojo shouted, "There they are!"

Sure enough, they were the next passengers down the plank, and Mrs. Morgan took off at a run. She gathered them up in a tearful embrace that they met in kind. The Bests stood off to the side for a few moments, letting the family have their time, then when Mrs. Morgan beckoned, they approached with smiles. Daniel gave his friends strong hugs, and he, too had tears in his eyes. Both young men greeted Mr. and Mrs. Best with gratitude and love, then Jojo received a big hug, too. Belle stood there waiting, and when they saw her, Adam stepped to her, threw an arm around her waist and kissed her full on the mouth. When he turned her loose, she was so surprised and overwhelmed she could hardly think. She was rattled further when Jeremiah did the same thing! Both Mrs. Best and Mrs. Morgan were staring at the two as if they'd lost their minds. Belle certainly had trouble finding hers.

Mrs. Morgan snapped at her sons, "What is the matter with you two?!"

Only then did Belle see the change in them. The dancing light had gone out of their eyes. They were thin and tired-looking, and the borrowed clothes fit badly. The kidnapping and its terrible aftermath had done something to them.

Adam apologized. "Beg pardon, Belle. We promised ourselves we'd do that as soon as we got back. It's what kept us going."

Belle didn't know what to say to such a declaration. It was quite apparent they'd not had a good time of it. "No apologies needed. We're all just glad you're here and safe."

Mr. Best cleared his throat and said, "I know you two have been through an ordeal, but if you ever treat Belle like that again, you'll be visiting my woodshed."

Mrs. Morgan added, "And I'll be providing the wood."

Both Morgan brothers nodded their understanding, but their smiles were thin, not the full, careless grins they wore before Watson altered their lives.

Daniel asked, "How about a welcome-home party? Are you two up to one?"

Jeremiah replied, "Sure, why not? Might be fun, but make it next week. Give us time to get our sea legs back."

"And the smell of the pens out of our skin," Adam cracked bitterly.

Belle knew all about slave pens. They were stocked with slaves destined for the public auction block, but mostly held the old, the dying and the desperate. They were filthy, miserable places. Her mother had languished in one for two months before a buyer could be found.

As everyone prepared to leave, good-byes and hugs were exchanged. It was a bittersweet reunion, and when it was over they all went home.

Later that evening, up in Belle's room, Jojo was slowly leafing through the dress plates featured in the latest edition of the *Godey's Lady's Book*. "You know, Belle, if two men ever kissed me the way those woodenheads kissed you, I'd've probably swooned right under the train."

"It was rather overpowering," Belle admitted. For someone who'd never been kissed before last week, Belle had them coming at her in droves it seemed.

Jojo asked then, "Who was the best kisser, Adam or Jeremiah?"

Belle was flabbergasted by the question. "Jo?!"

"What? It was just a question."

"Pretty personal, don't you think?"

"We're girlfriends, Belle. We're supposed to tell each other everything."

Belle chuckled. "Oh, really?"

"Yes," Jojo replied insistently.

"I have to admit, we are girlfriends, but—"

"But what?"

"I still can't answer your question because I don't know which one kissed the best."

"Why not?"

Belle shrugged and confessed. "I don't have a lot to compare them with, I guess."

Jojo admitted, "Me either."

Jojo leaned back on the bed and looked up at the ceiling for a moment, and asked, "Belle, what kind of man do you want to marry?"

Belle leaned back and looked up, too. She thought for a bit, then said, "Someone who's nice and loves me." Belle turned her head and eyed Jojo. "What about you?"

"I want him to be handsome, strong and kind. Sort of like Papa."

Belle smiled. Mr. Best would be an ideal model.

Jojo added, "Even though he and Mama disagree sometimes, they always kiss and make up. I like that."

Belle did, too.

Jojo said, "I think Dani would be much happier if he was going to marry you, Belle."

Belle sat up, but she didn't say anything.

Jojo asked, "You are sweet on him, aren't you—and lightning will strike you if you lie, Belle."

Belle grinned. "Your brother's right. You are a pest."

Jojo rolled over and propped herself up on an elbow. "Never mind that, just answer the question."

"The answer is yes, and if you tell him I said that, I'll sew all your curling irons to your hair while you're sleeping."

"He likes you, too."

"As a friend."

"As more than a friend. I may be only twelve, but I'm not blind. I've seen the way he's been watching you lately."

"But he's going to marry Francine, remember?"

Jojo shrugged. "There is that, but then maybe a miracle will happen. They happen all the time in those books Mama reads. The heroine faces all kinds of trials and tribulations, but always winds up with the right gentleman in the end."

"I don't think real life is that tidy, Jo."

"Well, not for women like us, but it doesn't mean it can't happen, does it?"

"No, Jo. It doesn't."

"Then I say, Francine the Queen will be swept off to Kingdom Come in a giant snowstorm, and you and Dani will get married."

Belle looked at Jojo and just shook her head. "You are something, Miss Josephine Best."

"I know, and soon, you're going to be my sister-in-law."

Belle couldn't do anything but laugh.

fourteen

The homecoming party for Adam and Jeremiah turned out to be an outdoor affair and was held at the Best home during the third weekend of June. Daniel and Mr. Best set up trestle tables, while Belle and Mrs. Best took shifts seeing to the food. Bea Meldrum contributed a bunch of chickens she'd received in payment for some healing she'd done, and once the birds were readied and seasoned, the pieces were set atop the grill manned by Mr. Best and Daniel. It seemed the whole community stopped by, bringing food, neighborly news and well wishes to Mrs. Morgan and her sons. There were sack races, horseshoe tossing and card games. Old men slapped dominoes, and young men eyed the well-dressed young ladies.

Francine and her entourage arrived late that afternoon. Belle didn't pay them much attention because she and Mrs. Best were too busy attending to the needs of the guests. Belle did garner a particularly haughty stare from the Queen though, but ignored it.

Belle was in the kitchen taking some of her famous biscuits out of the oven when Jojo and her friend, Trudy Carr, came in.

Jojo announced sarcastically, "The Queen's here."

Belle set the hot pan on the counter. "I know, she sneered at me when I walked by."

Trudy added, "Mr. Hood just arrived, too."

Belle began buttering the hot pieces of bread. There was so much to do, she didn't have time to be a part of the gossip. "Jo, will you take these out and set them on the table? Trudy, grab that pot of jam."

"Sure, Belle."

Belle turned to hand Jo the tray, but paused upon seeing Francine and a few of her friends coming in the kitchen's back door.

Francine, dressed all in green today, trilled, "Belle, be a dear and find me some thread. I snagged my hem."

Belle gave Jo the tray. "Thanks, Jo. Thanks, Trudy."

The girls exited.

Belle then turned to Francine. "I don't have time, Francine. I've a hundred things that need doing."

"This is important."

"So are these strawberries."

The church's reverend had brought over a basket full of the plump red berries. They needed washing and hulling before they could be enjoyed by the guests. Belle grabbed up the basket and headed to the door to take them to the pump, only to have Francine grab her by the arm.

"Did you hear me?" Francine asked, as if she were mistress and Belle her slave.

Belle slowly looked down at the hand on her arm, and then up into Francine's eyes. "Remove your hand."

"You will get me some thread."

Belle snatched free. "You will get out of my way."

"Who do you think you are?"

"I could ask you the same thing."

"Well, I'm your better, you ignorant little runaway. I'll bet you can't even read the word 'strawberry'!"

That hurt. "You'd be right, Francine. Now move before I show you just how ignorant I am."

Belle could see Jojo standing on the porch. Belle was sure she'd heard every word.

Francine had a nasty little smile on her face as she told her friends, "She actually thinks Dani likes her, as if he'd prefer an illiterate slave girl to me."

Belle forced her way past Francine and out the door.

Jojo stepped forward, but Belle, her eyes thick with furious, unshed tears, didn't slow. "Excuse me, Jo. I have to wash these berries."

The laughter of Francine and her girlfriends burned her back as she fled.

Under the pretense of allowing Mrs. Best to enjoy the party, Belle spent the rest of the afternoon and the early evening managing the kitchen, but as darkness fell, she slipped out for some solitude behind the barn. There were a few folks still celebrating, but she doubted they'd miss her presence. She despondently plopped down on the log bench Daniel and his father used for their work breaks. Alone for the first time since her confrontation with Francine, Belle let the tears fall. She was angry, hurt, and for the first time since coming to live here, ashamed of her past. Francine was right; she couldn't read the word *strawberry,* or even her own name, for that matter. She now understood what Mrs. Best had been trying to explain. The Francines of the world were unkind, and being uneducated gave them only one more stick to help build their fires.

"Belle?"

It was Daniel.

Belle stood and quickly turned her back, hoping he wouldn't see she'd been crying.

He could.

"Hello, Daniel."

"Hello. I've been looking for you. Jo told me what happened."

"Jo's got a big mouth," Belle said with a watery laugh.

"Are you all right?"

"No. No, I'm not." She turned back to face him. "Will you teach me to read?"

Daniel scanned her for a moment. He sensed the seriousness behind the request and knew there was only one answer he could give. "Yes."

"Tonight," she said firmly.

He chuckled. "How about in the morning? By the time everyone leaves—"

"Tonight, Daniel."

Daniel quieted. He sensed her anger and determination. "Sure, Belle. Whatever you want," he told her softly.

She turned away. "I never want to hear myself called an ignorant, illiterate slave ever again."

His lips thinned. Promise or no promise, he was through with Francine. How could she be so cruel? Belle had never hurt anyone. In fact, she'd gone out of her way to be as helpful and as nice as she could. "Do you want me to sit with you?"

Belle shook her head. "No. You go on back. I need to be by myself for a bit."

Daniel didn't want to leave. He wanted to stay and comfort her, hold her until the hurt passed and her smile returned. "I'll see you later then?"

"Okay."

After he departed, Belle sat alone in the dark, but she wasn't alone for long.

"Belle?"

Belle looked up. It was Mrs. Best.

"Hello," Belle replied.

Mrs. Best came and sat beside her. "Jo told me what happened."

"Lord, who didn't she tell?"

"Don't be upset with her. She loves you very much, and she was real angry with Francine. I had to send her in the house just now."

"Why?"

"Wouldn't stay out of Francine's face. Caused quite a scene, actually. Even made up a story about Francine making time with the teacher, Mr. Hood."

"She didn't make that up."

Mrs. Best went absolutely still. "What do you mean?"

"According to Jo and Trudy, Francine's been hanging on Mr. Hood since he arrived. Brings him lunch. They've even seen the two kissing."

Mrs. Best stared. "Are you sure?"

Belle shrugged. "As much as I can be. Jo doesn't like Francine, but she's not the kind of girl to go around making up things. She didn't want to tell Daniel or you, so she told me. It was keeping her awake at night."

"Why didn't Jo tell me?"

"She thought you'd turn Francine into stone."

Mrs. Best chuckled. "That child knows her mama well."

They both smiled. Mrs. Best draped an arm across Belle's shoulder and pulled her close. She kissed Belle's forehead. "You know," Cecilia said, "folks like Francine and her friends will be with you until you die. All you can do is improve yourself as much as you can, and then hold your head high."

Mrs. Best pulled back a bit so she could see Belle's face. "I know she hurt you, but you can't run and hide. Not you. You walked all the way from Kentucky, young lady—that shows strength, fortitude and determination. Don't you dare let gnats like Francine make you doubt your worth. We are all precious in His sight, and Lord knows, you're terribly precious in mine."

Belle was crying again.

Mrs. Best opened her arms and enfolded Belle with more love than Belle ever knew existed in the whole wide world. Mrs. Best whispered, "We love you very much, Miss Belle. Don't ever forget that."

As Belle's tears ran down her face, she thought about what Jojo said about her mama's hugs. Jojo was right; her mama's hugs were wonderful.

A few moments later, after blowing her nose on Mrs. Best's clean handkerchief and composing herself again, Belle declared, "The first thing I want to do is to learn to read. Daniel said he'd help."

"That's my girl. We'll all help. When shall we begin?"

"I told Daniel tonight, but I'm calmer now. We can start tomorrow."

"Good. Learning to read is the first step in improving yourself and in fighting back against all the Francines."

"Well, I'm ready to arm myself."

Mrs. Best nodded approvingly, then said, "In the meantime, what in the world do I do with this news about Francine and Mr. Hood?"

Belle shrugged. "Did Daniel hear Jo's accusations?"

"No, he was out walking the Morgans to their carriage, but everyone else still there certainly did. Won't be long before someone tells him."

"Do you think he'll believe them?"

"I don't know," Cecilia replied truthfully. "He's been talking of marrying that girl since he was fourteen."

Belle longed to reveal the promise Daniel had made to Francine's drying mother, but because he'd asked her to keep his secret, Belle kept quiet on the matter.

Mrs. Best stood. "Well, I won't meddle unless it becomes absolutely necessary. Daniel will come to me or his father if he needs guidance."

She looked down at Belle. "All of our guests are gone home now, so how about we head back to the house and see if Jo's still sputtering? Trudy's spending the night. I'm hoping that will give my hotheaded daughter something to do besides plot Francine's demise."

Belle chuckled. "Jo's a loyal friend."

"That she is, and Francine's going to think twice before taking her on again. Jo went at her like a terrier. Even though as a parent I had to send her to her room, I was very proud. Very proud."

The laughing women struck out for the house.

Once upstairs, Belle stuck her head around Jojo's partially closed bedroom door. "Knock, knock," she called out.

Both girls looked up with grins. Jojo was doing Trudy's hair. The room was thick with the smell of the smoky curling irons. Jojo asked, "How are you, Belle?"

"Much better. I just came to say thanks for standing up for me."

Jojo said bitterly, "She's a witch."

Trudy added excitedly, "Oh, Belle, you should've seen

the Queen's face when Jojo dropped Mr. Hood's name into the conversation. She went still as a post. I thought she was going to wither up and blow away."

Jojo took up the tale. "Then she tried to call me a liar, but—"

Trudy giggled. "The damage was done."

Jojo set more hair in the curler. "We think Mr. Hood stayed around because he was hoping to see Francine home, but when his name came up, he hotfooted it back to his horse so fast, you'd've thought he had Watson on his tail."

Belle chuckled. "Sounds like I missed a good one."

Trudy agreed. "Oh, you did. I'll bet the Queen won't have anything to say to Jojo after this."

Jojo added sagely, "Not unless she wants more of her business spread."

Belle shook her head with amusement. "Remind me never to get on your bad side, Josephine Best."

Jojo smiled. "No danger of that, Belle. Belle's going to be my new sister-in-law, isn't she, Trudy?"

"Sure is," Trudy agreed happily.

A laughing Belle rolled her eyes. "I'll see you two in the morning. Good night."

"Good night," both girls called back.

Belle headed down the hall to her own room.

True to his word, later that night Daniel knocked on Belle's door, ready to begin her reading lessons.

"Come in," she called.

He opened the door to find the room empty and dark but for a small light from a lamp on the stand beside her bed. Then he saw her standing outside on the small porch attached to her room. "Belle?" he questioned softly.

She turned. "Hi, Daniel."

"How are you?"

"Okay. Come join me."

Daniel crossed her room, then walked outside to stand beside her at the thick wood railing.

The stars were out, and the night was filled with the call of crickets. She said, "The warmer it gets outside, the more I enjoy this porch."

"My grandmother always did. Papa built it for her when she got too sick to come downstairs. I remember her reading to me out here. Then as I got older, I'd read to her."

"I didn't know my grandmother," Belle confessed. "Was yours as kind as grandmothers are supposed to be?"

"Kind and fiery. She was Papa's mama, and a Tory."

"What's a Tory?"

"Someone who supported the British during America's War for Independence."

"I know a little about that. July fourth, right?"

"Right. Only we in the North don't celebrate that day."

Belle was confused. "Why not? It's my favorite holiday. All the fireworks and the food."

"How can a country celebrate its independence while keeping three million souls captive?"

She now understood. "Never thought about it in those terms."

"We celebrate August first instead."

"Why August first?"

"Because on August first, 1834, the British freed its slaves in the West Indies. It was the beginning of slavery's end in Great Britain, and abolitionists everywhere celebrated. Now it's a holiday. There are parades and picnics and rallies all over the country."

"But no July fourth?"

"Not for us, no."

Belle thought on that for a moment. "I guess there are always two sides to things."

Daniel nodded.

Belle looked up at the sky. It was such a beautiful night. "Are there books that can tell me the names of the stars?"

"Yes."

"The only one I know is the Freedom Star." Belle scanned the sky until she found the constellation she knew as the Drinking Gourd. "There." And she pointed at the star they'd followed North. She wondered if her father was following it North right now.

Daniel nodded. "The North Star's one of the only ones I know, too."

"Really?" Belle was surprised. "I always thought you knew a lot about everything."

"I'm flattered, but nobody can know everything. It's impossible."

"Why?"

"There's too much to learn. Most folks concentrate on learning school things first, like reading and mathematics, and then more about the things they really like. Stars, for instance."

"I see. So maybe, once I learn to read, I could go on and learn everything I can about sewing?"

"I don't see why not."

Belle found that interesting.

"Did you still wish to begin tonight?"

She shook her head. "No. It's been a pretty long day. I was real upset when I asked you earlier, but I'm better now. How about tomorrow, after church?"

"Whatever you want."

"Tomorrow."

"Okay," he agreed. Silence settled between them again, then a few moments later Daniel asked, "Did you hear about Jojo going at it with Francine?"

Belle answered carefully. "I heard bits and pieces. I wasn't there, though."

"One of Mama's friends was, and she said Jo accused Francine of seeing the new teacher behind my back."

"Really?" Belle answered, hoping she sounded innocent enough.

"Yes."

"Do you think it's true?"

He shrugged. "I know Jo and Franny don't get along, but Jojo wouldn't make up something like that."

"No, she wouldn't."

He shook his head. "She's a pest sometimes, but she isn't a liar."

"And so?"

"So?" He shrugged again.

Belle's heart went out to him. "Did you speak with Francine?"

"No, she was gone by the time I got back from walking the Morgans to their carriage. They both said to tell you good-bye, by the way, and thanks for all the biscuits."

"They're welcome."

Daniel continued his chain of thought. "Francine leaving was probably best, though. After that mess with you, I wasn't speaking to her anyway."

Belle was glad to hear that. "So what are you going to do?"

"Tell her I don't want to marry her anymore."

Belle studied his face as well as she could in the dark. "Are you sure?"

He nodded. "Yes."

"Don't you want to give her a chance to tell her side?"

"I've tried, but every time I go by her house, Hodges says she's not home. Two plus two is always four, Belle. No matter how you add it up."

"I'm sorry it worked out this way, Daniel."

He didn't reply. "In a way, I am, too, but in a way, I'm not."

Their eyes met, and all those unspoken words and feelings returned. Belle wondered what would happen now that Francine no longer stood between them. When he leaned her way and kissed her softly on the forehead, the sweet feeling made her eyes close.

"Thanks for listening, Belle. I'll see you in the morning. Good night."

For Belle, the kiss coupled with seeing him draped against the stars made her wish he would stay, but she knew it wasn't proper for them to be out here this way, so she whispered back, "Good night, Daniel."

And he was gone.

The next afternoon, on the ride home from church, Belle received further news of her father. According to the communications received by the committee, he'd been moved to a safer location, just as Mr. Best predicted. In the month since his escape, the conductors in Ohio were slowly bringing him North, but because slave-catcher gangs were still prowling the main roads from Dayton to Toledo, a direct route to Michigan was out of the question, so he had to be taken Northeast first to avoid detection.

As Mr. Best drove them over the bumpy road, he told Belle, "At last report they're heading to Ashtabula."

Belle asked, "Where is that?"

"Northeast Ohio," Mrs. Best replied. "We lovingly call Ashtabula Mother Hubbard's Cupboard."

Belle thought it a funny name. "Why?"

"After a conductor there—a White man named Colonel William Hubbard."

Daniel told her, "Ashtabula's one of the safest hiding places on the road. The folks there take abolition very seriously."

His father added, "The newspaper there once declared, 'The voice of the people is, Constitution or no Constitution, law or no law, no fugitive slave can be taken from the soil of Ashtabula County back to slavery.'"

Daniel finished the quote, "And—if anyone doubts this real sentiment, they can easily test it."

Belle was impressed.

Jojo smiled Belle's way before asking her father, "Where will Belle's papa go after that?"

"Well," her father said, "they'll probably put him on a steamer and take him to Canada first, then he'll come here."

Belle asked, "A steamer?"

"Yes, we've a few lake captains working for our side. In fact, Colonel Hubbard has a tunnel that runs from his barn to the shore of Lake Erie and he rows his freight out to the ships."

Belle never knew the tendrils of the Underground Railroad extended even out to the water. Where would escaped slaves be without the help of so many people of all races? "So do you have any idea how long it will be before I see him?"

Mr. Best replied, "Truthfully, no."

Belle tried not to let her disappointment show. After all, her father was alive and, so far, still free. She knew the conductors were moving him along as quickly and as safely as they could, but Lord, she wished they'd hurry so she could see with her own eyes that he was alive and well.

fifteen

After the return from church, Daniel and Belle began her lessons. It was a nice warm June afternoon so they took advantage of the weather and sat in the sun on the steps of the back porch. Once they were comfortable, Daniel put a sheaf of paper atop a thin, book-sized piece of wood, and began to print a series of letters.

Belle watched. "What's it say?" she asked curiously.

"Belle Palmer," he told her. He showed it to her, then pointed out each letter. "B-E-L-L-E P-A-L-M-E-R."

Belle took the wood from his hand and closely examined what he'd written on the paper. None of the curves and stick figures meant a thing. "I've never seen my name before."

When she looked up, Daniel wondered if she knew how beautiful she was. "Well, that's what it looks like. Hand me the board back."

Belle did, then looked on as he made a lot more sticks and curves. He told her, "This is the alphabet. There are twenty-six letters, and they make up all the letters in all the words."

"Only twenty-six. For some reason, I imagined there'd be many more."

"Nope. Just twenty-six."

He handed her the board. Belle took a moment to look at the twenty-six letters, and then told Daniel firmly, "I can do this."

His eyes shone with approval. "I don't doubt it for a minute."

So for the next few days, Belle spent all of her time working with the letters of the alphabet, and practiced printing her name. Everyone in the Best household pitched in to help, but all stayed within the parameters of Daniel's prepared lessons. In reality, he was the most educated person in the family. His Oberlin certificate made him amply qualified to teach, and so everyone deferred to him as to how best to teach Belle.

By the end of June, Belle had all the letters memorized, and could call them out by sight. Mrs. Best refused to let her do any housework, saying Belle had a more important job to do. No amount of protesting from Belle would make Cecilia change her mind, so Belle gave up and went back to her lessons.

A few days later, Daniel was out at the pump washing off the sawdust when he saw Belle running toward him. She was waving a piece of paper and calling excitedly. Smiling because she seemed so happy, he waited for her approach. When she got near enough, she stuck the paper in his face. "Look, I did it. All by myself!"

Daniel saw that she'd written her name. *Belle Palmer.* The letters were a bit crude, but that didn't matter; she'd get better. He smiled proudly. "Congratulations. Did you show this to Mama?"

"No. I wanted you to see it first."

She looked ecstatic and he felt the same way. Next thing he knew, she threw her arms around his neck and kissed him soundly on the cheek. "Thank you, Daniel. Thank you so much! I have to go show your mother."

In a flash of blue skirts she was gone. Daniel, bowled over by the fact that she'd kissed him, watched her flight with a smile in his eyes and in his heart.

The month of June slid into the warm hot, hazy days of July, and just as Daniel predicted, July fourth was not celebrated. It passed as just another day. By mid-July, Belle was ready to tackle the basic rudiments of reading. She found it much harder than printing or learning the alphabet because it all seemed so confusing. Take the letter *e*, for instance. Belle couldn't understand why it did so many things to so many words. It could turn *tap* into *tape* and *hop* into *hope*. When it stood beside the letter *i*, it had the power to turn *nice* into *niece*, and sometimes, it made the letter *y* take its place, as in the words *early* and *curly*. Belle found all the rules and the exceptions to the rules frustrating. She was disheartened at times, but she didn't give up.

Daniel enlisted the Morgan brothers to help with Belle's classical education. Before opening the area's general store, their mother and late father had been teachers in Canada and thus had a very extensive library. The Morgans had books that opened Belle's world to famous works of art and to people in faraway lands. They read her fables and myths, sonnets and limericks. Learning with them was fun for Belle but she couldn't help but notice that neither of the brothers was as playful or as happy-go-lucky as he'd been before their kidnapping.

At the end of one of their sessions, Belle walked Jeremiah back to the wagon parked in front of the house.

He'd come alone today. Adam had stayed to help at the store. "Thanks again," she told him as he climbed up into the seat.

"You're welcome." Jeremiah picked up the reins. He looked down at Belle. "Can I ask you something?"

He seemed so serious, and his eyes were so bleak, Belle nodded. "Yes."

"How'd you survive it?"

She knew what he meant. Slavery. "I didn't know anything else."

He looked off into the distance. "Adam and I couldn't bear it for even two days. They took our clothes, our shoes. We were put on the block with nothing on, and handled as if we were animals."

Belle's lips tightened sympathetically.

He went silent then and Belle could only imagine the degradation he must be remembering. "You're home safe now, Jeremiah."

"But it could happen again," he told her. "Watson could break into our home and drag us off and—"

He seemed to shake himself back to the present. "I'm sorry, Belle. I didn't mean to burden you with my troubles."

"It's all right. We're friends, remember?"

He gave her a ghost of a smile. "You were our light. Adam kept saying to me, 'Belle did this for sixteen years, and survived. We can, too.'"

"And you did," she pointed out softly.

He shrugged. "I'm still having nightmares. Half-grown man, having nightmares like a child."

"That's nothing to be ashamed of."

"I suppose," he replied. "Well, let me get on home. I'll see you in a few days."

"All right."

As he drove away, Belle watched until he disappeared from sight.

When Daniel had gone by Francine's house a few days after the Morgans' homecoming party, he'd been informed by Hodges that she and her father were gone to Windsor to visit friends, and wouldn't return for a month. Daniel found that quite convenient, but he'd thanked Hodges and left. Now the month was up. According to rumor, she'd returned last night.

Hodges let him in, and directed him to the well-furnished drawing room.

At his entrance, Francine, all in blue, stood and smiled. "Hello, darling." She came to him and placed her arms around his waist. "Give me a kiss so I'll know you missed me."

Daniel looked down into her eyes, and said quietly, "Tell me about you and Hood."

Her gaze went chasing off. "I'm not sure what you mean."

"Rumors are going around saying you two are sparking."

Francine backed away. Her voice was cool. "Your sister has never liked me—"

"This has nothing to do with Jo. Is it true?"

Daniel could see her gauging his mood and whether she could get away with fabricating a reply. He knew her well because he'd known her a long time.

"It's this way, Daniel. Paul and I—well, I think I'm in love with him."

Daniel's jaw tightened. So it was true. He felt like a fool. "Then I hope you'll be happy."

"Oh, Dani, don't look like that. If this doesn't work out, you know I'll be back."

"But I won't want you back."

She stared. "Daniel?!"

"Francine, what do you think this is? I'm not going to wait around to see if you and Hood work out."

"Well, why not?"

"Self-respect, Francine. Do you know what that is?"

Her lips thinned. "It's that little runaway, isn't it?"

"Belle didn't cause this. You did."

"You do like her, don't you?"

"And what if I do?"

"She's an ignorant—"

The anger in his face stopped her. Francine didn't finish the sentence. She said instead, "Then I suppose there's nothing left for us to talk about. Hodges will show you out."

Daniel left gladly.

When Daniel returned home, his parents were sitting on the front porch watching the fiery sunset.

"How's Francine?" his father asked him.

"Who cares."

Cecilia raised an eyebrow. "Did you two fall out?"

"She says she's in love with Paul Hood, but if it doesn't work out, she'll come back to me."

Mr. Best began to chuckle sarcastically. "That girl needs a switch taken to her selfish little behind."

Mrs. Best could only gape at what she'd heard. When she finally found her voice, she stood and said angrily, "William, get the wagon. We're going over there, and when I get my hands—"

Mr. Best laughed in earnest. "Sit down, lovey. We're not going anywhere. I don't have any bail money if you kill her. Daniel took care of things, I'm sure."

His mother asked sharply, "Did you?"

Daniel shrugged. "I suppose."

Cecilia's heart ached seeing the angry hurt in her son's eyes. She wanted to roast Francine. "Sweetheart, if you need to talk—"

"I'm all right, Mama. I'll see you later."

He went into the house.

Having Jojo as a friend meant that for the next week Belle heard all the rumors surrounding the breakup of Daniel and Francine. Some claimed Francine had given Daniel the mitten, while others swore it had been the other way around. Jojo and Trudy had ears like bloodhounds, it seemed, because every day when Jojo returned from school, she clued Belle in on the latest whispers. In reality, Belle didn't care; all she had to do was look at Daniel's tight face to know that regardless of who initiated the dissolution, Daniel didn't seem happy to be in the center of it all. Belle put up with Jojo's news though, solely because Jojo was twelve, and at twelve the only excitement she had in her life was gossip, going to church and school.

But by the fourth day, Belle had had enough. "Jojo, that's it. No more rumors."

"But, Belle, what if it's true?" Jojo replied with scandalous glee.

Belle looked up from her reading primer and gave Jo a steely look. "Francine is not carrying Mr. Hood's love child. She may be fast, but she's not stupid."

"But, Belle, Trudy heard—"

Belle closed her book and declared calmly, "Josephine Best, I don't care if she heard it from a talking frog. I don't want to know any more."

Jo looked crushed. Belle felt a pang in response, but all this gossip and these rumors had to stop. "Jo, think of how

Daniel feels to have his name swirling around in this mess. You of all people know how hard this has been on him."

Jo admitted grudgingly, "I do."

"Then help him out, please. No more carrying tales."

"All right, but—Francine *is* breeding. Just wait. You'll see."

After Jojo's departure, an amused Belle shook her head. Daniel was right. His sister was a pest.

In the week that followed, Daniel moved through the house like a ghost. Belle saw him at meals and occasionally during the day, but he never had much to say. He spent most of his time working in the barn with his father, and the rest at the home of the Morgan brothers.

On this particular morning, Belle and Mrs. Best were sorting through some donated clothes collected by the women of Mrs. Best's female antislavery circle. According to her, the group had been in existence since the thirties, ministering to the sick and shut in, collecting clothes for runaways and even managing stations on the Road. The clothes they were looking over now were headed across the Detroit River to some fugitive-aid organizations in Windsor and Amherstburg, Ontario.

As they worked they chatted, and Belle asked, "Do you think Daniel's ever going to smile again?"

Cecilia shrugged. "All I know is, if his jaw gets any tighter it's going to shatter."

Belle agreed as she searched for holes in the pair of trousers in her hands. "Well, I hope he comes back to himself soon. Haven't whipped him at checkers in quite some time."

Mrs. Best grinned.

Meanwhile, out in the barn, Daniel put down his

plane and said to his father, "Can I talk to you about something?"

Mr. Best glanced up from the table he was working on. "Sure, son. What about?"

"Women."

"Ah," Mr. Best replied sagely, "how about we take a short break?"

Daniel nodded. So they went out to the log behind the barn and took a seat.

Mr. Best asked, "So what do you want to know?"

"I'm pretty sure I'm in love with Belle."

Mr. Best stared. "I thought this was going to be about Francine."

Daniel shook his head. "Nope. Belle. Frankly, I'm glad Francine gave me an out. Now I can court Belle."

His father said, "Let me get this straight. All this moping you've been doing—"

"I'm not moping, Pa. I'm angry—at Francine, Hood, but mostly at myself for letting Francine turn me into the county laughingstock. I thought I was in love with her because she'd always been there, but I had nothing to compare true, deep-down feelings with. Now I do."

His father studied him silently, then asked, "And your plans with Belle are what?"

"I'd like to court her, Papa."

"No."

Daniel's eyes went wide. "No?!"

"No," his father repeated quietly. "You spent the last three years claiming to be so deeply in love with Francine, you wanted to marry her."

"But—"

His father cut him off. "And now that you're no longer in love with her, you claim to be in love with Belle."

"Why, yes, and—"

"What if, say in six weeks or six days, you decide you no longer love Belle? It would be pretty awkward around here with the two of you living under the same roof, don't you think?"

"Yes, Papa, but—"

"Do you have any idea what your mother would do to you if you broke Belle's heart?"

"I've a pretty good idea, yes, but—"

"You may be her firstborn, but she'd grill you like a piece of pork."

Daniel didn't know whether to be offended or to grin.

"Son, what I'm saying is, it's too soon. Give yourself some time before you go charging into something new. Lord knows, I've been hoping you'd send that Francine packing for years, and I'd love to have Belle as my daughter-in-law, nearly as much as your mother would, but I want it to be lasting. I don't want either of you hurt. Do you understand?"

Daniel didn't necessarily agree, but he did understand. "May I at least take her places—rallies, the theater—"

"If you take your sister along."

Daniel looked stunned. "Papa?!"

"Those are the conditions. Now, say by December, if your feelings are still strong, we can talk about a formal courtship. Until then, Belle will be allowed to see other young men, if she desires."

Daniel's eyes widened.

His father ignored it. "She's been here only three months, Daniel. She needs time to finish mastering her studies and to figure out who she's going to be. If you do love her, you'll give her the space she needs to grow."

This conversation had not gone in the direction Daniel had envisioned, but he knew his father was right. "Okay,

Papa, but if she picks one of the Morgans over me, I'm going to be real mad."

"Belle's smarter than that, and you know it."

Daniel smiled. He hoped to be as wise as his father when he had children of his own. "Thanks, Papa."

"Anytime, son," his father replied affectionately. "Anytime. Now, let's get back to work."

At dinner that evening, Daniel looked across the table at his sister, and said, "I'll do your dishes tonight, Jo."

Jojo looked very skeptical. "Why?"

"Because you're my sister, and I love you," he gritted out.

"Oh, you just want to be in the kitchen with Belle," Jojo stated with a twinkle in her brown eyes.

"Pest," he shot back.

Belle pretended to be concentrating on her collards. When she hazarded a look at Mrs. Best, she was smiling.

Mrs. Best then said to her son, "Taking Jo's chores tonight will be perfect, Daniel. She has a book she has to study tonight for a test tomorrow. Don't you, Josephine?"

Jo fiddled with the mashed potatoes on her plate. "Yes, but the book is dumb. I don't know why we have to read it. The boys don't."

"It's a book on female decorum," her mother pointed out.

"But it's written by a man, for heaven's sake."

Her mother cast her a warning look.

"I'm sorry, Mama, but I still don't see why I need it. You've already taught me all those things."

Her father asked, "What's the book called, Jo?"

Jojo recited in a singsong voice, *"How to Be a Lady—A Book for Girls Containing Useful Hints on the Formation of Character.* It's by a *man* named Harvey Newcomb."

Belle chuckled softly and shook her head. "I'd like to read it, Jo, once you're done."

"You're welcome to it. Tomorrow we're having a test on the chapter titles."

Daniel asked curiously, "Not the contents?"

"No, that will be next week, maybe, Mr. Hood said. I don't think he's a very good teacher."

Mr. Best asked, "Why not?"

"He doesn't teach us anything. We just do a lot of reading, so he can—"

She hazarded a glance Daniel's way but didn't say more.

Mrs. Best looked down the table at her daughter. "So he can what?"

Jojo shook her head. "Never mind. Nothing."

Her mother pressed her. "Jo, if there's something not right with his teaching, the parents need to know. Now, tell me, darling."

Jojo looked over at her brother, and then back to her mother before saying, "We don't see very much of him."

Mr. Best looked as confused as everyone else at the table. "What does that mean?" he asked.

It was obvious Jojo didn't want to confess, but she had no choice. "Ever since we moved school into the church basement, he gives us a lesson to read when we arrive, and then we don't see him again until lunch. Then, after lunch, he gives us another reading assignment, and we don't see him again until it's time to go home."

Mrs. Best practically shouted, "What?"

Jojo's lips were tight.

Mr. Best demanded, "Is it liquor? Does he come back smelling like spirits?"

Jojo shook her head. "No, he comes back smelling like Francine."

Belle choked on the drink of water she'd just taken. Daniel handed her a napkin.

Mrs. Best then asked, "Is this every day?"

"Yes, ma'am."

Mr. and Mrs. Best exchanged a look, then he pushed back from the table, saying, "Lovey, we're paying too much money for shenanigans. Bad enough he's fooling around with Francine. Now this? I'm going over to talk to Walt."

Walt Fleming was the head of the local school committee and Francine's father.

Mrs. Best didn't try to dissuade him from his mission. "I agree. If Hood is foolish enough to want Francine, fine, but we're paying him to teach."

"Let's hope Walt views it that way."

A very disgruntled Mr. Best left the house.

After his departure, Belle and the other family members finished dinner, then cleared the table. Mrs. Best went up to Jojo's room to help her with the memorizing for the upcoming test, while Belle and Daniel headed for the kitchen.

Belle washed. Daniel dried. As they moved about the small kitchen, both tried to ignore their awareness of each other. Daniel put the now-dried plates into the sideboard, then asked, "Are we done?"

Belle looked around the tidy kitchen, and said proudly, "Yes, we are."

"Then will you come sit on the steps with me? Something I want to talk to you about."

Belle took off her apron and hung it on the peg by the stove. "Sure, what is it?"

"Us."

Belle went still. She searched his eyes, then forced herself to say calmly, "All right, Daniel."

Outside, the sun was going down on what had been a

very windy July day. Belle took a seat on the stone step, and he sat down at her side. Belle was admittedly nervous.

Daniel didn't beat around the bush. "I asked my father if I could court you."

Belle started shaking. "I didn't know you were going to do that. What did he say?"

"No."

Belle stared. "No?"

"No."

"Did he have a reason?"

"Yes, he wants you to finish adjusting to being here, and for me to wait until I'm sure how I really feel about you."

"How do you think you feel?"

"You know how I feel, Belle," he told her quietly. "If you were older, I think I'd just marry you."

Belle almost fell off the porch. "Marry? Me?!" she croaked.

"Yes, marry." He peered into her face. "Would that be all right?"

She was absolutely speechless. "You'd really want to marry me?"

"Yes, but you didn't answer me. How do you feel about me?"

Belle forced herself to speak slowly. "I'd marry you, Daniel." She gave him a cautious glance and found him smiling.

He leaned close. "May I kiss you?"

Belle's eyes closed, and she was shaking so badly she just knew she was going to fly apart. She looked up into his eyes and nodded her permission. The kiss was even more splendid than the last time he kissed her, that night Mr. and Mrs. Best went to the ball. Belle had no idea what she was supposed to do, so she just let herself feel. His lips were warm, soft. She sensed her breathing increasing and felt a warm tingling take root inside. Next she knew, he was easing them closer. Her hand came up to cup the back of his head and the kiss deepened. Her mouth parted. He nibbled on her bottom lip and Belle pulled back. Panting, she brought her trembling hand to her lips. Daniel's eyes seemed to be the whole world.

He told her softly, "I'm sorry. Am I going too fast?"

Belle whispered, "I think so."

Just like last time, she wanted him to kiss her again, but the force of the moment was still charging through her, echoing like church bells. Shaken, Belle said, "I should go in now, Daniel.

"Whatever you want."

She stood, but was unable to pull her eyes from his eyes, his mouth. "I'll see you later."

He nodded, then said, "Belle?"

She looked down into his eyes again. "Yes."

"We'll go very slowly, all right?"

She nodded. "All right." She fled into the house.

Up in her room, Belle stood with her back against the door. Daniel wanted to marry her! Her, the former slave. She'd no idea kisses could be so moving. Still reeling, she brought her hands to her lips. They were swollen and puffy. Knowing how they got that way immediately floated her back to being in his arms. She wanted to tell the world how happy she was, wanted to jump up and down, holler, scream; but instead, she melted back against the door and smiled contentedly.

sixteen

Instead of going to school the next day, Jo and her classmates and their parents were summoned to a meeting at the church. The children were cross-examined by the school committee about the recent goings-on in the classroom. Each child told a tale similar to the one Jojo had told at the dinner table: Mr. Hood would disappear for hours on end, returning only long enough to give them another reading assignment or to dismiss them for the day.

"Then what happened?" Belle asked Jo as they sat outside shelling peas for dinner. Belle hadn't gone to the meeting and so had to rely on Jojo for the details.

"The adults sent us out of the room. They called Mr. Hood in and were in there for maybe a quarter of an hour."

Belle raised an eyebrow. "That long?" she asked sarcastically.

Jojo shrugged. "Well, what could Mr. Hood say? He was caught like a pig in a fence. He couldn't call us all liars."

"So what did they decide?"

"The adults voted fourteen to nothing to have him removed. He was fired a minute later."

Belle shook her head. "I hope Francine was worth it."

Jojo cracked, "I doubt it."

Belle could see Daniel over by the barn putting the tack on the team. They hadn't had any private time since last evening on the porch. The idea that he might love her and want her as his wife still seemed like a dream, and the thought made her giddy all over again.

Jojo could see Belle's interest in her brother and so asked, "Are the two of you rowing in the same direction now?"

Belle swung her eyes to Jojo and just smiled.

"Hallelujah! It's about time. Wait until I tell Trudy."

Belle warned, "You are not to tell Miss Trudy anything. Daniel and I haven't committed to anything yet."

"But—"

"No buts. We've only agreed to liking each other, that's it. Your father wants me to finish my education and settle in a bit more, and he's right. Who knows, maybe I'll want to go to Oberlin before everything's said and done."

Jojo grinned. "Wouldn't that be wonderful, Belle? You at Oberlin? Oh, we would be so proud."

Belle knew she would love Jojo forever. Not once had Jo done anything but share and support Belle's dreams for the future. "That would be something, wouldn't it?"

Belle watched Daniel and his father load a large clock onto the bed of the wagon, then secure it with rope. "Where are they taking that?"

"Back to the reverend. He needed the glass in the front replaced."

Belle heard Jo, but her eyes and mind were on Daniel. She gazed at him for so long, Jo finally said, "Belle, we can stay out here and gaze at my brother for the rest of the day, but I think Mama wants these peas for tonight's dinner."

Belle started, then, smiling, said, "I was not thinking about your brother."

Jo didn't believe her for a moment. "Lies like that will make lightning strike you, Belle Palmer."

Both girls laughed and went back to the peas.

That evening, Belle settled into a chair in her room to do her nightly reading. Due to all the time and effort she'd put in, she'd improved enough to no longer be frustrated by all the rules and sounds of the letters. As a result, she was tackling bigger words and feeling very proud of herself. She couldn't read particularly fast, but she was faster than she'd been last week and knew she'd be faster in the weeks to come. Naturally she wanted to be proficient now, this minute, but it wasn't realistic, so she plodded on.

At midnight, she rubbed her tired eyes and pushed her books aside. She stood and slowly stretched her tired back and limbs. Time to go to bed, she told herself. As she walked over to her ancient armoire to take out her night-clothes, the sound of something hitting the porch outside made her slow. Rain? Belle walked over to the open door and out onto the small porch. To her surprise, there on the ground stood Daniel. "Daniel?"

He immediately placed his fingers against his lips, signaling quiet.

She giggled silently. What in the world was he doing out at this hour?

He picked up a ladder hidden in the grass by the darkness and quietly placed it against the porch. He looked up at her in the moonlight. Belle's eyes widened. Surely he didn't mean for her to climb down? As if sensing her hesitation, he made a show of putting his hands together in a silent plea.

She giggled again. The idea was certainly tempting. She'd been wanting to see him all day. Her mind made up, she held up one finger, signaling him to wait, then hurried quietly back into her room and doused the lamp. Sneaking out of the house in the middle of the night was bad enough; she didn't want to leave the lamp lit and burn the place down, too.

Belle returned to the porch. Daniel smiled up at her when she came back into sight, and she grinned down in reply. He moved to brace his weight against the ladder. Once he was ready, Belle hiked up her hem, and slowly and carefully climbed down to the ground.

On solid ground now, she whispered, "Hello."

"Hello, yourself," he replied, smiling. "Come on."

Hand in hand, they ran happily but quietly to the bench behind the barn.

After they were seated, Daniel confessed, "I've never done anything like this before." He looked her over. "I missed you today."

"I missed you, too."

Belle knew what was coming next. The kiss they shared set off fireworks inside her again. When he eased back, Belle felt like she was floating up with the stars. "Your papa's going to take a switch to both of us...."

"Probably..." Daniel whispered, then kissed her again.

They fed themselves on kisses for a long while, savoring this new love, but Daniel could feel himself wanting more than just her kisses, so he slowly, reluctantly pulled away. Belle was an innocent; he knew he couldn't do with her the things he'd done with Francine, no matter how much he wanted to. He hoped to make Belle his wife someday and because of that he respected her enough to wait.

Breathing hard, Daniel leaned back with his head against the barn wall and tried to will himself back to a calmer state.

"Are you all right?" Belle asked with some concern.

He shook his head. "Nope, and probably won't be until our wedding night."

Belle's eyes widened. "Daniel!" she whispered, scandalized.

"Hey, it's the truth."

Belle had never been so embarrassed in her whole life. "Let's talk about something else."

He chuckled. "All right. Don't think it's going to help me, though."

"Daniel!"

He gave her a crooked grin. "Sorry."

She laughed then, too. "This is all so new."

"I know it is. That's why I'm sitting over here, and you're over there."

Belle confessed, "I don't really know that much about—any of this."

"I know. Maybe you should talk to Mama."

Belle wasn't sure. "I don't know, Daniel."

"Mama or Jo, those are your choice."

Belle chuckled. "That does narrow it down, doesn't it?"

"A mite."

Belle still found it hard to believe this magnificent man wanted her: Belle Palmer, runaway. "I feel like I'm in a dream, and if I wake up, I'll go back to being plain old Belle, and you'll go back to being Francine's intended."

He looked her in the eyes and made it clear. "Francine and I are done. Over. If she wants Paul Hood she can have him."

"Are you sure?"

He nodded solemnly. "Yes. Do you think I'd risk my father's wrath this way if I wasn't sure? I've never snuck a woman out at night before in my life. Never."

Belle supposed he had a point. Being with him made her feel so special. All she wanted to do was smile.

In the moonlit silence surrounding them, the call of the crickets played on the night air like a hushed symphony. Belle reached out and gently touched his face, slowly stroking her fingers down his cheeks. He covered her hand with his, then tenderly kissed her fingertips. Feeling bold, Belle leaned in and softly pressed her lips to his. Once again, the time passed unnoticed, and then finally Daniel eased away. Belle's eyes were closed. Her heart was beating so fast she didn't think it would ever slow down again.

Daniel knew the sooner he got her back to the safety of her room, the safer she'd be. She was entirely too tempting to be out here with him in the moonlight; he was a male after all, and sometimes males didn't think clearly in situations such as these. He closed his eyes and tried to shift his mind to less volatile thoughts, but all he could focus on was her sweet mouth. Daniel wondered if his father knew how hard this was going to be. How in the world was he expected to wait until Belle reached eighteen? He turned his head her way.

Belle met his gaze. "What?" she asked softly.

"Do you know how beautiful you are?"

Belle dropped her gaze. "But I'm not."

He reached out and gently raised her chin so he could feed himself on her glittering, coal-black eyes. "You are very beautiful, Belle Palmer. Very," he echoed.

Belle began to shake all over again. Her voice came out a whisper. "We should get back...."

"I know..." he agreed, but he kissed her instead.

A little while later, they crept back across the grass to the house. After a quick kiss good-bye, Belle climbed the ladder to her room. Once she was safely on the porch, she blew him a kiss, then went inside.

Belle was more than a bit tired when she came down to breakfast that next morning, but seeing Daniel seated at the table made her forget all about how sleepy she was, and she smiled.

"Good morning, everyone," she said as she took her customary seat next to Jo. As Mr. Best began to say grace, Belle slid Daniel a look from beneath her lashes. He flashed her a wink. Belle's responding smile died when she realized Mrs. Best was looking right at her. Belle immediately dropped her gaze and concentrated on Mr. Best's voice.

When the grace was finished, the family began passing the food back and forth, and Mrs. Best said to Belle, "You look a bit tired this morning, dear."

Belle took the platter of eggs from Mrs. Best's hand. "I was up late." Belle replied, hoping Mrs. Best didn't possess mind reading as one of her many mama talents.

Mrs. Best warned, "Well, no burning the late-night oil tonight. You need your rest, dear."

"Yes, ma'am."

"And I need to talk with you about something later on, all right?"

Belle had no idea what it might be about, but said, "Yes, ma'am."

"Is Belle in trouble, Mama?" Jojo asked around a mouthful of sausage.

Cecilia replied, "No, but you may be, if you keep talking with your mouth full."

Everyone smiled. Even Jojo. "Sorry, Mama."

"And besides," Mrs. Best continued, "even if Belle were in trouble, you'd be the last person I'd let know. You and

Trudy would have Belle's business spread so fast, our heads would spin."

Belle looked over to see Mr. Best grinning. He said, "Maybe they'll grow up and be newspaperwomen like Mary Ann Shadd, up in Canada."

Mrs. Best cracked, "And maybe by then they won't have to sign their editorials with a man's name like Mary had to."

Belle stared, confused.

Daniel must have seen her confusion because he explained, "Mary Shadd was the first woman on the North American continent to publish her own paper, but because she didn't believe the male subscribers would pay attention to the words of a woman, she signed all of her editorials with a false male name."

"Is she a Colored woman?" Belle asked.

Mrs. Best said proudly, "Yes, she is. Her father was a well-known Road conductor in Pennsylvania." Then she added, "But what those male abolitionists put her through with her paper—"

An amused Mr. Best said, "Oh, Lord, here we go. Daniel, why'd you get her started on this? You know how she gets. Next, she'll be sputtering about Fred Douglass and *that* woman."

Belle assumed that to be a reference to Mr. Douglass's mistress, Julia Griffiths.

Mrs. Best looked over at her husband. "I hope he isn't planning on bringing her with him when he comes to visit next month."

The now chuckling Mr. Best shook his head. "With the way you women have been howling all over the country about this? I think he has better sense, and from what I hear he may not come after all. Too busy. Besides, he and Miss Griffiths have gone their separate ways."

Mrs. Best didn't appear to believe that. "It's just such a slap in the face to his wife, Mary, that's all. All those years she spent raising those children alone and trying to keep a roof over their head while he was off in England lecturing and gallivanting."

Mr. Best said, "I know, lovey, but getting all upset about it won't change things. Besides, there's no real proof of shenanigans."

Mrs. Best shot her husband such a hard look, Belle thought he'd be turned to stone.

He simply laughed. "I love it when you've got fire in your eyes."

Mrs. Best smiled, seemingly in spite of herself. "Oh, eat your eggs," she said finally.

He threw her a bold wink and proceeded to do just that.

Watching their interplay, Belle hoped to have a marriage just like the Bests. When she glanced over at Daniel to gauge his reaction to his parents' teasing play, he met her eyes with a knowing smile.

Trudy and her papa came over later that afternoon. Since formal schooling had been canceled until another teacher could be found, the two girls were going to spend a few days together at Trudy's house. It took Jojo nearly a half hour to gather up what she needed for the stay. Most of it was hair gadgets and irons.

Once they departed, Belle cleaned up the kitchen, then searched out Mrs. Best. She found her in the garden, on her knees weeding her collards.

Belle said, "You said you wished to speak with me?"

"Yes, let's get out of this sun, though." She stood and

wiped her brow. The July day was a particularly warm one. They went and sat on the shade-covered back porch steps.

Mrs. Best began. "Mr. Best has been approached by a very nice young man from the church. He wants to call on you."

Bell croaked, "Me?"

"Yes. Why not you?"

Belle thought about Daniel. "Well, I—"

"He's very nice, Belle. He and his parents moved here from Illinois about three years ago."

Belle couldn't think of anything to say.

Mrs. Best asked, "A bit speechless, are you?"

Belle didn't lie. "A bit, yes."

"So, do you wish for him to call?"

Belle thought about Daniel once again. "What's his name?"

"Bertram Brown."

For the life of her, Belle couldn't remember ever seeing this Bertram Brown at church or being introduced to him. "Mrs. Best, I'm not sure—"

"Dear, no one wants to rush you into anything. If you don't want him to come calling, just say so."

"I don't—I mean, I'm very flattered, but—"

"It's all right, Belle," Mrs. Best offered reassuringly. "If you're not ready, you're not ready. Maybe in a few months' time."

Belle nodded, then asked, "Was there anything else?"

"No, dear. That was all."

"Do you want me to help you weed?"

"No, you go back to your studies."

"Yes, ma'am."

Belle headed to the house. Had she glanced back, she would've seen the pleased smile on Cecilia's face.

* * *

At midnight, Daniel came calling again, and Belle happily answered. Leaving her room, she quietly climbed down the ladder. Laughing and in love, they ran to the bench behind the barn. The kisses started before either of them could speak: tender, lingering kisses, filled with the rush of welcome. They knew they didn't have much time; forty minutes, an hour at the most, then they'd have to slip back.

Belle said against his lips, "Your parents are going to kill us."

Daniel kissed her back. "As long as they put us in the same grave, we'll be fine."

Belle laughed softly and he did, as well.

He took a seat on the bench, then with a gentle tug on her hand, directed her onto his lap. Belle felt a bit awkward, but when she looked up, he was smiling. She confessed, "Can you tell I've never sat on a boy's lap before?"

"I can," he replied. Her back was as stiff and straight as a piece of Michigan pine. Hoping to ease her nervousness, Daniel softly moved his hand up and down her robe-covered back. "Just want to have you near, Belle, that's all..." he whispered. "Lean in so I can feel you against my heart...."

His hushed invitation gave Belle such a case of the trembles, she almost jumped up and ran, but this was Daniel, *her* Daniel, and she wanted to be held against his heart. Swallowing her jitters, she cuddled close and let herself be enfolded in his arms.

Once she was settled, and the silence of the night returned, he kissed the top of her hair. "This isn't so bad, is it?"

She shook her head. "No." And it wasn't. It was wonderful. She felt treasured, sheltered. With him by her side, she had no worries.

Daniel thought it wonderful, too. In some ways, a bit too wonderful. Belle was so soft and warm against him, he had to take in a series of long, deep breaths in an effort to slow down his body's natural reaction. All he kept thinking about was how long this next year and a half was going to be. "When's your birthday?" he asked, hoping such an innocent subject might help calm him.

She shrugged. "Sometime this summer. I never knew the date."

"You should pick one."

Belle leaned back so she could see his face. "Can I do that?"

"Papa does it all the time when he forges papers. If a runaway can have a new name, why not a birthday?"

"When's yours?"

"October twenty-sixth."

"And you'll be?"

"Nineteen."

Belle rested her head against his chest. "Then I'll pick August the first."

He peered down at her. Why?"

"Because of what you told me about it. Having a birthday on a day when so many slaves were freed seems perfect."

"Not to mention folks all over the world will be celebrating that day. Good way to have a lot of parties thrown on your behalf."

Belle smiled against his heart. "There is that, too."

"Then August first it will be."

"Thank you, Daniel."

He gave her a tight hug. "You're welcome."

They sat, content.

A little while later, they knew their time together had

come to a close. Daniel asked from above her, "May I walk you home, miss?"

"Is it that time already?"

He kissed her hair. "It is."

Belle looked up, and with a mock pout said, "But I don't want to go back."

He chuckled. "In a year or so you won't have to. We can sit like this until dawn."

Belle admitted she couldn't wait. "Do you really think we'll still like each other well enough to get married?"

He raised her chin. "I do."

"I do, too," she told him.

"Then we're agreed," he whispered softly and kissed her.

Belle got back into her room without mishap. She climbed into bed and fell asleep, smiling.

The next day Belle was so tired she could hardly hold her eyes open at breakfast. Daniel didn't look much better. After Mr. Best said the grace, Mrs. Best passed Belle the jam pot and said, "You know, the two of you would be rested come morning if you weren't going up and down ladders at night."

Belle froze.

Daniel spit coffee all over his eggs.

Mr. Best eyed them both grimly, but didn't say a word. He didn't have to.

Mrs. Best turned back to Belle and Daniel and asked, "Any questions?"

Both young people answered in unison: "No, ma'am."

So that was that; no more sneaking out at night to share kisses and dreams. Belle thought they'd gotten off lightly, or she hoped they had. Daniel did, as well. They could've easily been turned to stone.

seventeen

A week later, just as Mr. Best had predicted, the great Frederick Douglass canceled his visit to the area, citing other more pressing matters. Daniel was very disappointed by the news. Jojo's comment was, "You mean I spent all that time sewing on that stupid banner for no reason?"

By now, Belle's reading and penmanship had improved markedly, but neither skill was as proficiently performed as she would've liked, so she kept working by reading newspapers, magazines and antislavery pamphlets supplied by Daniel and his parents.

She was also sewing. Mrs. Best had been correct: the dress Belle had made her for the ball was the best bit of advertising Belle could have imagined. Belle had three gowns under way, and three more on order. She was so busy, she hardly had time to breathe, let alone figure out a way to sneak off and meet Daniel.

One evening after supper, Belle came to the Bests with a proposal: "I'd like to invest in a sewing machine."

They both looked surprised.

"A sewing machine?" Mrs. Best asked.

"Yes, here's an advertisement in the *Godey's Lady's Book*."

Mr. Best took the book from Belle's hand, then he and his wife read it. Mrs. Best asked Belle, "Did you see how much it will cost, dear?"

"Yes, ma'am, but it says I can pay over time at two dollars a week. I just have to send a little bit of money now."

Mrs. Best confessed, "I've never heard of such a thing, paying over time."

Belle hadn't either, but she was surprised they hadn't; she'd assumed this paying over time was a common practice here in the North.

Mrs. Best read a bit more. "It says here this Mr. Singer is the first businessman anywhere to offer a plan of this sort. Do you have any money saved, Belle?"

"Yes, ma'am, I do. Jojo's also offered to be an investor, and I can pay her back when my business improves."

Mr. Best chuckled. "You're going into business now?"

"Yes, sir, as soon as I can get the machine. I've more dresses to make than I can handle alone, so I thought a machine might help. That way I wouldn't have to turn anyone away."

Mrs. Best said, "Belle, I'm proud of you. I don't see why she can't order the machine, William, do you?"

Mr. Best shook his head. "Neither do I. As long as this Mr. Singer is a straight arrow, I say send him the money, Belle, and I'll make you a sign to put out front."

Belle stared. "Then it's all right?"

Mrs. Best looked puzzled. "Of course, dear."

Belle hastened over and gave each of them a hug. "Thank you, thank you, thank you," she chanted happily. She then ran up to her room to get started on her letter.

Daniel ended up writing the letter to the Singer Company on Belle's behalf because Belle thought his handwriting so much better than her own. Daniel posted the letter the next day. Belle was so excited she doubted she'd be able to sleep until after the machine arrived.

The next morning, Belle came down to breakfast to find Jojo eating at the table alone. Confused, she took a seat and asked, "Where's everyone?"

"Outside. Papa's taking Dani fishing."

"Fishing?"

"Yep."

"Where?"

"Canada."

"Canada?"

Jojo laughed. "You sound like one of those talking parrots I saw in Boston once when I was little. Just like you, it repeated everything a person said."

Belle ignored that. She instead went to the window that looked out over the side of the house. Sure enough, Daniel and his father were filling the wagon bed with gear. Mrs. Best was standing off on the side, supervising, it seemed. Belle asked Jo, "Do they go to Canada often?"

"Every few years or so, but Dani doesn't want to go this time. Papa's making him. I think they're going so they can talk."

"About what?"

Jojo popped a piece of muffin in her mouth. "Do Mama and Papa know that you and Dani were sneaking out at night?"

Belle remembered that Jojo had been at Trudy's the morning Mrs. Best put a stop to their midnight meetings. "How'd you know about that?"

"I heard you the first night. I thought it was so romantic," she added dreamily. "Who would've ever thought my brother could act like Romeo?"

"You heard us?"

"Sure. I'm right next door, remember, and if I heard you, I know Mama did. She's a very light sleeper." Jojo then asked again, "So do they know?"

Belle answered glumly, "Yes." She and Daniel had thought themselves so clever, but they hadn't been at all.

"Then that's probably why Papa's taking Dani fishing."

All Belle could think was that Daniel was in trouble because of her. She had to try and set things right. She hastened to the door.

Jojo called, "Where're you going?"

"I'll be back."

Outside, Mr. Best was seated atop the wagon, reins in hand. Daniel was seated at his side. When Belle ran up, she looked first at the unhappy Daniel and then at his father. "Mr. Best?" she said.

He nodded down at her. "Morning, Belle."

She hazarded a glance Mrs. Best's way, acknowledging her, before responding, "Good morning, sir." Then gathering her courage, added, "Sir, if you're going to punish Daniel for what we did, you should punish me, too. It was just as much my fault as his."

He paused for a moment to survey her, then asked, "Oh, so were you putting up ladders outside of his window in the middle of the night, too?"

Belle dropped her eyes. "No, sir."

"Then I guess you're not as much at fault."

Belle remained silent.

Mr. Best then told her, "Belle, I appreciate your willingness to share the blame. Daniel and I are going fishing because we have some talking to do—about a lot of things, but I'll bring him back in one piece. Don't worry."

Belle smiled.

Mrs. Best walked up, draped an arm around Belle's waist, and gave it an affectionate squeeze. "Tell them good-bye, Belle, dear. They need to be going."

Belle looked up at Mr. Best, and said, "Good-bye. Have a good time."

Then she turned to Daniel. "Bye, Daniel."

He gave her a small smile. "Bye, Belle."

As the wagon pulled away from the house, Belle's heart missed him already.

On August the first, Belle awakened at dawn to the knowledge that it was her birthday. She sat up. She hadn't told anyone else in the Best family that she'd chosen this day on the calendar to mark her birth; only Daniel knew. Most of the folks in the community were going over to Canada today to celebrate the historic August First. Belle was looking forward to the trip, not only because it was a holiday, but because Daniel and his father were planning to meet them there.

Daniel had been gone five days now: five days without his smile; five days without his encouragement; five days without seeing him when she wanted. Jojo said absence makes the heart grow stronger. Belle didn't agree.

To celebrate the holiday, the Best women were going to drive over to Canada with the Morgan brothers and their mother, then ride home with Daniel and his father. When the Morgans arrived, they helped load all the food, quilts and other paraphernalia needed for the out-of-doors celebration onto the wagon. By 7 A.M. they were on their way to Detroit.

They reached the docks a bit after half past eight, and Belle couldn't believe the sheer number of people waiting to be ferried across the Detroit River to the Canadian shore.

Looking around in wonder, she remarked, "I never imagined there'd be so many people."

As Adam eased the team into the ferry line, Mrs. Best said, "This is a small crowd really. In Harrisburg, Ohio, back in '49, two thousand folks came together for August First. Blacks and Whites."

There weren't two thousand people here today, but Belle would be willing to bet there were several hundred. Everywhere she looked she saw black and brown faces of all shapes and sizes and in all manner of dress. She saw well-dressed families and families dressed in rags. Many of the celebrants were children; others were elderly; some were in large church groups, while a few sat atop their wagons all alone. Just as Mrs. Best had noted, there was also a smattering of White abolitionists in the crowd. Out on the river, a small flotilla of canoes and rafts filled with passengers headed downstream to the Amherstburg docks. According to Mrs. Best and Mrs. Morgan, the main gathering would be held on a farm not far from there. Amherstburg had a sizable fugitive and Canadian Black population, and many on the docks hoped to be reunited with friends and family.

As Adam moved the team up a spot in the line, Mrs. Best added, "There are probably quite a few runaways hidden in with the crowd, too. A group this large provides a perfect opportunity to move freight, and with so many people here, no slave catcher in his right mind would dare start a search."

Jeremiah cracked bitterly, "Not unless they want to be found floating in the river later."

That didn't mean the slave catchers weren't in attendance, though; they were. Belle spotted the mounted Otis Watson and a few of his dirty-skinned men watching ominously from the fringes of the crowd. The evil grin on

Watson's cadaverous face sent chills up Belle's spine. She didn't look his way again.

An hour or so later, after ferrying across the Detroit River, the Best party drove onto the farm where the celebration was taking place. Speakers were up on the makeshift podium, and hundreds of people were seated on the grass, atop quilts and old blankets, listening raptly. Once Adam found a place to park, his passengers carried all their belongings to a spot nearby. With their mothers' blessings, the young people took off to explore, but Belle kept looking around for Daniel. She couldn't wait to see him again.

The tables of food appeared to be a mile long. Cakes, cookies, and all manner of dishes wrapped in cloths and newspaper were on display and would be eaten later. The area was cordoned off by rope to ensure there would be no nibbling ahead of time, so Jojo and Belle handed their food contributions to one of the smiling, white-dressed women keeping watch, as did Adam and Jeremiah.

The annual parade had already begun by the time they made their way across the field, but they did get to view most of it. Belle once again marveled at all the people, and at the procession of antislavery-society members carrying colorful banners passing by the applauding and enthusiastic onlookers. First came the Canadian contingents representing societies in St. Catharines, Niagara Falls and Buxton. The Americans came next, shouting slogans and singing songs. Groups from Battle Creek, Cleveland and Chicago passed by for review, as did folks from Dayton and Toledo, and an all-children clan from Detroit's Second Baptist Church.

After the parade, everyone drifted off to sample the other entertainment, such as the choir competition and the contests on the game field. Belle and Jojo laughed at the greased pig competition and were participants in the sack race. Jojo and Jeremiah won a ribbon. Belle and Adam came in next to last.

By late afternoon, they wove their way back to their blanket, and much to Belle's delight, there stood Mrs. Best talking with Mr. Best, and Daniel was standing beside them. When he glanced up and saw Belle, she couldn't decide whose smile was bigger. Lord knew, she wanted to run and throw her arms around him, but in such a public place with hundreds of folks milling about, she had to settle for the smile.

"Hi, pest," Daniel said, greeting his sister first.

"Hi, yourself. Did you catch a lot of fish?"

"Sure did."

He smiled Adam and Jeremiah's way, then finally turned his eyes on Belle. Everything Daniel felt for her rushed to fill his heart. "Hello, Belle."

"Hello, Daniel. I—we missed you."

Jojo cracked, "Speak for yourself."

The Morgan brothers laughed.

Without taking his eyes from Belle, Daniel asked his sister, "Isn't there somebody here who needs their hair done?"

Jojo, seeing that they only had eyes for each other, said, "I can take a hint. I'm going."

"Good," Daniel told her.

Belle looked up to find Mr. and Mrs. Best and all the Morgans watching. She found the scrutiny highly embarrassing.

Mr. Best said, "Daniel, why don't you take Belle over to hear some of the speakers?"

Daniel didn't have to be told twice. Hiding his exuberance, he asked Belle. "Would you like to go?"

Her happiness equaled his, but she forced herself to respond calmly. "Sure."

And off they went.

Belle couldn't tell who spoke or what they spoke about.

All she knew was that she and Daniel were together again, and for her, nothing else mattered.

They were standing at the back of the crowd surrounding the podiums when Daniel reached into his pocket. "I have something for you."

The gift was small and wrapped in tissue paper. A happy Belle took it from his hand. When she opened the paper, she found a small, gold-colored locket inside. "Oh, Daniel." She gasped softly as she held it up. "It's beautiful."

"Happy birthday."

Belle went still. This was the first birthday gift she'd ever received in her seventeen years on earth, and the magnitude of what the little locket represented brought tears to her eyes.

Daniel saw the waterworks, and said, "Aw, Belle, why are you crying? You know I don't like it when you cry."

Without thinking past his desire to comfort her, Daniel pulled her into his arms and held her tight. "What's wrong?"

"I've never had a birthday present before, Daniel, that's all."

He hugged her tighter. He vowed right then and there to make the rest of her birthdays as memorable as he could.

As they made the walk back to the spot where they'd left his family, Belle asked, "Did you and your father talk?"

Daniel nodded.

When he didn't volunteer anything further, Belle asked, "Well, what did he say? Are you—we—still in trouble?"

"No. Not unless we sneak out again. Papa fussed a bit, but he said he was young once, too."

Belle smiled. She was certainly glad there hadn't been any serious repercussions. She was just about to ask Daniel where in Canada he and his father had gone fishing when she noticed people running. Daniel did, too. To Belle it seemed as if the entire gathering were in flight.

A man ran past them. Daniel grabbed his arm. "Friend, what's happening?"

"Slave catchers!" the man related hastily, then hurried on. Belle's eyes widened.

Daniel grabbed her hand. "Come on!"

Daniel knew that if slave catchers were indeed on the hunt, he had to get Belle back to his folks. They'd protect her with their lives if need be. Hand in hand they ran against the flow of people back to the spot where they'd left his parents. They arrived just as Mr. Best was pulling his long gun from beneath the tarp on the wagon. Adam and Jere were already armed. Their faces were angry.

Mrs. Best cried, "Oh, thank goodness, you're back."

Daniel asked, "What's this about slave catchers?"

His father answered tersely, "Watson's trying to take some men back over the border."

"But his writ has no value here; this is Canada!"

"Try telling him that," his father returned.

Mr. Best tossed Daniel a rifle. "Let's go."

Mr. Best then turned to his wife, and said very seriously, "Lovey, you and Mrs. Morgan stay here with the girls."

Mrs. Best protested, "I can shoot as well as any man here, William."

"I know that, but stay put. We'll be back."

And off they ran.

Mrs. Best looked at her companions and said testily, "Well, I guess he told me. As if women all over the North haven't been dispatching slave catchers, too!"

When Jojo heard that, she said warningly, "Mama, you heard Papa."

Mrs. Best told her daughter, "Yes, I did, but your father knew I wasn't an obedient wife when he married me. Let's go. We may not have bullets but we can throw rocks."

Mrs. Morgan added, "And he can't possibly believe I'm going to sit here and knit while that cur Watson steals another mother's sons. I'm right behind you, Cecilia."

So the women hurried off in the direction the men had gone. Belle had to admit, she hadn't wanted to wait around for the men to return and report either. Who knew how many catchers were involved and how much help the men might need.

The ladies arrived on the outskirts of a crowd that numbered in the hundreds: men, women, children, all buzzing angrily. In the center was the mounted Watson and three of his men. Ringing them were at least two dozen abolitionist men, Black and White, all with guns drawn and pointed his way. Because there were so many people, Belle couldn't see who Watson had in his clutches, but she wondered if the slave catcher had lost his mind. Did he really believe he'd be able to take someone back to slavery in the face of such armed resistance?

Apparently, he did, because he barked, "Y'all back away before someone gets hurt!"

Mr. Best's voice rose over the crowd. "The only people hurt are going to be you and your men, Watson. Ride away. You've lost this one."

"The hell I have. I have a writ here from the sovereign state of Georgia."

"This ain't Georgia!" someone reminded him.

The tension rose. The catchers' mounts began acting skittish and nervous. Watson's men were having difficulty keeping the animals still.

Mr. Best's voice rose again. "Let them go!" The buzzing of the crowd took on an ominous tone. Belle still couldn't see Mr. Best or Daniel. She did see many women, especially those with children, begin to hustle away. They were moving to safety. The air was thick with danger. Belle prayed Watson would come to his senses before bedlam erupted.

Suddenly, a shot rang out in the distance and everyone turned to see three men riding hard toward the crowd. Folks began to cheer, but Belle didn't know why.

"It's the local lawmen," Mrs. Best explained. "Someone must've ridden for them at the outset. Now we'll see what Watson has to say."

Watson had panic on his face. Yanking his reins around, he attempted to flee, but a dark hand grabbed the bit and held on. Other hands, Black and White, shot out to detain his men by similar means. Chaos erupted. The catchers were determined to get away. The abolitionists were equally as determined to make them stay.

Then a series of shots rang out overhead and everyone stilled. The Canadian lawmen had arrived on the scene and it had been their guns firing. The crowd parted to let the men into the circle. Following Mrs. Best's lead, Belle tried to move closer to the front. Her view of who Watson was trying to take back was still blocked, but she could see the happenings on horseback.

The Canadians had evidently run into Watson before because one man said, "Well, well, if it isn't our old friend, Mr. Watson."

Watson sneered.

The lawman tossed back a menacing smile. "Sneer all you want, but you were warned last year not to bring your evil pursuits to the Queen's shores again, yet here you are."

"I've a writ," snarled Watson.

"Let's see it."

Seemingly pleased that the lawman appeared to be entertaining his side of the argument, Watson flashed the crowd a triumphant, black-toothed grin. They responded with catcalls as he reached inside his filthy coat and extracted a folded sheaf of papers wrapped in oilcloth and tied with a string. As the catcalls continued to rain down, Watson calmly untied the package and handed the Canadian the writ.

The lawman spent a scant ten seconds perusing the document, then before God and everybody tore the paper to shreds and let the pieces blow away in the wind.

A joyous roar erupted from the crowd. Watson's eyes bulged with fury. Belle's grin met that of Jojo.

The Canadian then told Watson, "You and your men are under arrest for trespassing, mayhem and threatening the lives of Canadian citizens. You can come willingly or I can deputize every man here and they can help us subdue you."

Watson scoffed. "We're citizens of the United States—you can't arrest us."

"If you were on American soil, you'd be right, but this land belongs to Her Majesty Queen Victoria, and by the authority vested in me through her, you'll be lucky if you see America ever again. You were warned, Watson."

Another roar went up. Watson was livid but he knew he had no choice. He could either cooperate of his own free will or the lawmen, with the assistance of the crowd, would make him cooperate. In the end he tossed down his gun, and his men followed suit.

The lawmen made the slave catchers dismount, tied their hands with thick rope, and marched them back the way they'd come. Applause filled the air. The now happy assemblage began to disperse and the faces of the men Watson had been threatening were finally revealed. Belle took one look, went stone still, and then screamed happily, "Papa! Papa!" And she took off at a run.

eighteen

At the sound of her voice, James Palmer turned. The sight of his daughter bearing down on him filled his dark face with first shock and then joy.

Running so fast she couldn't even see the surprise on the faces of her friends, Belle was already crying as she launched herself into her father's outstretched arms.

"Oh, Papa! Papa! You're all right!"

James Palmer cried, too. In a voice thick with emotion, he whispered, "I thought I'd never find you again."

They held on to each other, rocking and crying. The Bests and Morgans looked on with tears in their own eyes.

A very moved Daniel studied the man and realized that Belle resembled her papa quite a bit. Both were tall and dark. Belle had his bright black eyes, but his face was sharper, his jaw more pronounced. Belle was thin, but her father was muscular, as big and strong-looking as the bricks he laid for a living.

A sobbing Belle held on to her father for all she was worth for fear of losing him again. After a good long while, she stepped back and wiped away her tears. Taking her father by the hand, she led him over to the people she'd come to love just as much.

"Papa, I want you to meet Mr. and Mrs. Best. I've been living with them since we were separated, and they've treated me just like their own. Mr. and Mrs. Best, my papa, James Palmer."

Mrs. Best was still crying, so her husband stepped up and firmly shook the outstretched hand. "Glad to meet you, Mr. Palmer—real glad to meet you. You've quite a girl there. We've enjoyed her."

"Thank you for looking after her. I'll always owe you."

Belle then introduced the Morgan brothers and their mother. They greeted Mr. Palmer warmly. Adam said with great sincerity, "We've learned what it means to be free from your daughter, sir. Welcome home."

Jojo came next and Belle said, "Papa, if I ever have a sister, I want her to be just like Jo. This is Josephine Best. She's helped me an awful lot since I've been here."

"Hello, Josephine."

Jojo nodded. Her tears of joy were evident in her brown eyes. "Hello, Mr. Palmer. I'm so glad you're finally here."

Then it was Daniel's turn. Belle said, "And this is Daniel Best. Jo's brother, and their son. He was the one who found me, Papa. He's also helped me learn to read."

Her father stared at Belle and his grin was wide. "Really?"

Belle nodded.

James Palmer shook Daniel's hand with a firmness that relayed his gratitude. "Thanks, son. Thanks very much."

Belle couldn't believe her papa was actually by her side. She no longer had to worry if he was safe or wonder where he was, or if he was alive. She now had the answers to all of those questions and she wouldn't have to worry about him ever again.

When it was time to return home, the wagons were loaded and the Morgans and the Bests joined the long line of buggies, wagons and carriages snaking their way back to the docks where the ferries waited to transport them back to America. Jojo, seated next to her brother in the crowded wagon bed, was slumped against his shoulder asleep even before they got to the docks. They were all tired but filled with the excitement of finding James Palmer.

On the night ride home, James answered as many questions as he could about his ordeal since seeing Belle last. Initially, he had been captured in Michigan by Watson's men, and yes, he did escape from Watson's friend Boyle.

He explained further, "Once me and the others found a safe house, we slept by day and moved North by night. We never would've made it, though, if we hadn't had those conductors with us. They fed us, clothed us, kept us safe. They kept telling us we'd be free at the end of the journey, but there were days when I didn't think the journey would ever end."

Belle said, "But you knew I was still here in Michigan."

He smiled. "Yes. The brother of the lady conductor in Dayton told me he knew where you were and that you were still in Michigan, and safe. I knew then that if I persevered, I'd see you again. That kept me going."

Daniel asked, "So how did Watson become involved today?"

"He knew my face. He'd seen me in Michigan when I was first taken. The conductor who brought us to Canada planned to slip me and the others across the border when the celebration ended. They said it would be easy to do with so many folks traveling that way, but Watson and his men were riding by while we were eating and, as I said, he recognized me. I was awful glad to see everybody come to our aid though, and then to find my Belle—" Emotion seemed to fill him again, because he didn't say anything more. He simply gazed down at his daughter seated by his side, hugged her shoulders and kissed her forehead. "I'm so glad to see you."

Tears filled Belle's eyes again. The arm he had draped around her shoulder was real; he was real. She still found it hard to believe they'd been reunited or that when she got up in the morning his smile would be there to greet her. Belle looked over at Daniel seated on the other side of the wagon. She had his love and his locket around her neck, and now she had her papa back in her life. This August first would be a birthday she'd never forget. Never.

Daniel carried his sleeping sister up to Belle's room. Mrs. Best had decided Mr. Palmer would have Jo's room for now.

James Palmer began to protest. "Mrs. Best, don't you have a barn or something? I'll be perfectly fine out there. Josephine shouldn't have to give up her bed for me."

Cecilia Best looked him in the eyes and said, "I'd think you'd be tired of sleeping in cold, damp barns, James Palmer."

Mrs. Best turned to Belle and said, "Belle, dear, show your father upstairs."

Mr. Palmer opened his mouth to further protest, but William Best said with a chuckle, "Mr. Palmer, you'll learn it's best to just follow along. Save yourself a lot of grief that way."

James asked, "You sure?"

"Positive. Been married to her over twenty years."

Belle chimed in. "He's right, Papa. No one wins many arguments with her."

James smiled and shook his head. "Okay, Mrs. Best, upstairs it will be."

Cecilia looked pleased. "Good. Belle will show you the way."

Once Belle and her papa were alone in the room, they shared another long hug of greeting. He said softly above her hair, "Wish your mother was here."

"I know. Maybe once we get you settled in, we can ask Mr. Best and the Vigilance Committee if they can find out where she is."

"You think they can?"

"I'm sure they'd try if we asked."

"Then we'll do that."

He drew back and looked at Belle. "So, tell me everything that's happened since I saw you last, and how long you've been sweet on Mr. Daniel Best."

Belle's eyes widened with surprise. "Papa! How'd you know?"

"I wasn't sure till just now."

Belle's mouth opened as wide as her eyes. "Papa?!"

He laughed. "Heard it in your voice when you introduced him. Saw it in the shine in your eyes."

A smiling and embarrassed Belle dropped her head. "Is it that obvious?"

"A blind pig could see it," he teased.

So he and Belle sat. They talked well into the night and long after everyone else had gone to sleep.

The next few days were spent getting James Palmer acclimated to his new surroundings. Mrs. Best let him sleep as much as he needed to in order to regain his strength, and Belle spent most of his waking hours just marveling at his presence. When she wasn't making sure he was all right, she and Jojo spent the rest of the time working on a very special surprise Belle planned to reveal when the time was right.

On Saturday, Mr. Best took Mr. Palmer to the weekly Vigilance Committee meeting. Mrs. Best and Jojo were inside the house finishing the hem on a dress Belle had recently made for Jojo, and Daniel and Belle were seated on the porch.

Daniel said, "Your father seems to be getting along okay."

"He is, isn't he? I'm still pinching myself to make sure I'm not dreaming and that he's truly, truly here."

Daniel was about to say more, but the sight of Francine's distinctive black coach pulling to a stop in front of the house made him go quiet. Belle recognized the coach right off, too.

Daniel said, "I wonder what she wants."

Belle cracked, "She probably wants you back, but she can't have you."

He grinned.

Francine swept up the walk in a voluminous ivory-colored cape. "Good evening, Daniel," she said frostily. She looked over at Belle, then baldly dismissed her before turning her attention back to Daniel.

Daniel recognized the slight for what it was, and it didn't improve his mood. "What do you want?"

"For both of us to come to our senses."

"I didn't realize mine had left me."

"Oh, darling, I know we've had our differences in the past, but—"

"Go home, Francine."

"But you don't understand—"

"Go home, Francine!"

Belle thought that any woman in her right mind would hear the finality in Daniel's voice, but not Francine the Queen. Nope, she had the nerve to get mad. "Daniel, I will not be shouted at."

He lowered his voice to a soft, sinister level. "How's this? Go. Home."

"I can't," she snapped angrily.

"Why not?"

She clawed open her cape. "This is why!"

Belle saw the small but distinctive swelling in Francine's belly and almost fell off the steps. Jojo and Trudy had been right. Francine *was* breeding!

Daniel looked stunned, as well.

Francine explained in a clipped voice. "Papa says I either find a husband or he'll ship me to his sister in Peoria."

"So what do you want from me?"

She looked at him as if he were addle-headed. "I want you to marry me, Daniel Best. You promised Mama you'd take care of me. Remember?"

Belle could feel anger stiffening her limbs.

Suddenly, the screen door opened. Mrs. Best stepped out. Belle moved aside to let her pass.

Cecilia said coolly, "Evening, Francine. I couldn't help but hear all this shouting. Is something wrong?"

It pleased Belle to see a tiny trace of fear creep into Francine's eyes.

"Oh, hello, Mrs. Best. No, nothing's wrong. Daniel and I—"

"Is my son the father of your child?"

Francine's gaze darted away. She didn't speak.

"Look at me," Mrs. Best demanded softly.

Francine slowly met her eyes.

"Is my son the father of your child?"

"No," Francine finally admitted, in a not-very-respectful voice. "But Daniel promised my mother on her *deathbed* that he'd take care of me—"

"FRANCINE!"

It was the first time Belle had ever seen anyone practically turned to stone. The full power of Mrs. Best's voice had frozen Francine like a statue. Belle felt a quiet movement behind her. She glanced back and saw Jojo grinning in the shadows.

Mrs. Best was now saying to Francine in a low, but furious voice, "How dare you come to my son carrying another man's child. Be glad that your mother's not here, because if she were, she'd slap your face. Now get back in that carriage, and take your shame elsewhere. Don't you ever darken this doorway ever again. Do you hear me?"

Francine's eyes swept Daniel's tight face, then after giving Belle and Mrs. Best a malevolent glare, Francine the Queen did as she was told. A few moments later, her coachman drove her away.

In the silent aftermath, the still angry Daniel looked to his mother, and said, "Thank you, Mama, but I could've handled her on my own."

She patted him on the back. "I know, and I'm sorry, but I've been wanting to do that for so long."

Mrs. Best then walked over and took Belle's cheeks between her palms. She placed a solemn kiss on Belle's forehead. As Belle's confusion showed on her face, Mrs. Best said quietly, "Thank you so much for coming into my son's life."

Belle looked over at Daniel. He appeared to agree.

Daniel spent Sunday afternoon after church fishing with the Morgan brothers. He didn't bring home any fish, but he did return home bearing some sad news. During dinner he told everyone that the Morgan family was moving back to St. Catharines in Ontario.

His mother asked, "But why?"

A solemn Daniel played with the peas on his plate. "Mrs. Morgan has an aunt there. She's very sick and needs someone to care for her, so they're leaving."

Jojo asked quietly, "When are they going?"

"Tomorrow morning, first thing. I guess Mrs. Morgan's very worried about her."

The sadness in Daniel's voice made Belle's heart ache. She knew how much the Morgans' friendship meant to him.

Jojo asked with hurt in her eyes, "Didn't they want to say good-bye?"

Daniel looked at his sister's devastated face, then explained gently. "They did, pest, but they didn't have time to tell everyone, so they're just going to leave. They sent everybody here their love, though, especially you."

Everyone appeared crestfallen.

Jo asked, "Do you think we'll ever see them again?"

"They promised to visit whenever they get the chance. So, yes, we'll see them again."

Later on, while Mr. Best took Belle's father to the shed to show him his tools, Belle went to look for Daniel. She thought he might need someone to talk to in the face of losing his best friends. She found him seated on the back porch alone. "I'm sorry your friends are leaving," she told him as she sat beside him.

"You know," he said, "I've known them since I was ten. We'd go hunting in the winter. Smelting in the spring..."

He quieted then as if remembering.

Belle said, "I'll miss them."

"So will I."

He reached down and took her hand in his. "I wonder if we'll see them again."

Belle liked holding hands with him. "They said they'd come visit when they could."

He looked over at her and asked softly, "Are you trying to make me feel better?"

Belle nodded. "Yes. Is that so bad?"

"No, it's very touching. Thanks."

He then looked around to see if they were being observed. Somewhat secure that they weren't, he leaned over and kissed her tenderly. Belle's love soared and she kissed him back just as tenderly. The kiss didn't last nearly as long as they would've wished, but with three adults now in the house, the young sweethearts couldn't afford to risk more.

Daniel kissed the back of her hand. "You should go on in. I'm going to sit awhile."

"I'll stay and sit if you'd like."

He shook his head. "If you stay we're going to get into trouble."

Belle smiled, then touched his cheek. "Okay."

"Good night," he said, his heart filled with love.

"Good night, Daniel."

Daniel was sitting alone under the stars when James Palmer walked up.

"Care if I join you?" Mr. Palmer asked him.

"No, sir."

Belle's father sat. For a moment the silence resettled, then he said, "Your pa's a good man. Says he wants to hire me, help me get on my feet."

Daniel thought that was good news. "Papa's been wanting to work with a good bricklayer for some time now."

"That's what he told me."

The silence came between them again, then James said, "Want to thank you again for finding Belle and bringing her to your folks."

"You're welcome."

"She thinks a lot of you and your family."

"We think highly of her, too."

"So, what are your intentions toward my Belle, son?"

Daniel knew the two of them were destined to have this conversation, but he hadn't been expecting it now, this minute. Gathering his thoughts, Daniel finally replied, "To marry her and love her for the rest of my life."

Mr. Palmer studied him closely, then said, "And if I let you marry her, when the time comes, how will you support her?"

"I can teach. I'm also a fairly good carpenter. Not as skilled as my father, of course, but I hope to be one day."

Mr. Palmer nodded approvingly. "Well, good night, Daniel."

A bit surprised that Belle's father hadn't had more to say, Daniel replied, "Good night, sir."

Daniel waited until Mr. Palmer disappeared into the house before releasing his pent-up breath.

nineteen

BY the end of August, Belle was ready to spring the surprise she and Jojo had been working on, so Sunday after church she and Jojo called everyone into the parlor and asked that they take a seat.

Her father did as the girls requested but asked, "Belle, what is this about?"

"A lot of things, Papa. You'll see in a few minutes."

He shrugged at Mr. and Mrs. Best and Daniel. They appeared curious, as well. Belle and Jojo took a moment to slip into the kitchen so they could talk privately.

Jojo asked, "Are you ready, Belle?"

"I think so."

"Then I will announce you, okay?"

Belle nodded.

Belle stood in the kitchen door while Jojo said with a flourish, "Presenting Miss Belle Palmer."

Belle stepped into the parlor and Jojo began to applaud. The rest of the audience took their cue from her and began to applaud, as well.

Belle said, "Thank you."

She then said, "Back in April, Daniel and Jojo found me on the side of the road and brought me here. Mr. and Mrs. Best took me in and nursed me, fed me. They gave me clothes and guidance and love."

Mrs. Best wiped at a tear.

"There's no way I can repay them for all I've seen and learned, so this is my small token to that enormous debt. This is also for my papa. He's paid a great price trying to ensure that I had a better life. Thank you, Papa."

Then in the silence that followed, Belle raised her voice and began to recite the poem that was the abolitionist anthem—Mrs. Best's favorite poem and now Belle's: *Bury Me in a Free Land*, by Frances Ellen Watkins.

> *Make me a grave where'er you will,*
> *In a lowly plain or a lofty hill;*
> *Make it among earth's humblest graves,*
> *But not in a land where men are slaves.*

> *I could not rest if around my grave*
> *I heard the steps of a trembling slave;*
> *His shadow above my silent tomb*
> *Would make it a place of fearful gloom.*

As Belle went through the next four verses, memories of her mother being sold on the block made her voice resonate with pain, but the listeners also heard her strength. By the time Belle began the eighth and final verse, everyone's eyes were filled with pride at this show of accomplishment. She'd come a long way from the illiterate fugitive she'd once been.

> *I ask no monument, proud and high,*
> *To arrest the gaze of the passers-by;*

All that my yearning spirit craves,
Is bury me not in a land of slaves.

When she finished, there were a few moments of silence, then her father rushed over and pulled her into his arms. Belle was crying and he had proud tears in his own eyes.

Wiping at his tears, James turned to the Bests. "How can I ever thank you?"

Mrs. Best said emotionally, "I believe Belle just did."

Belle went over to Mrs. Best, who enfolded her into her arms, and they both laughed and cried their joy. "I'm so very, very proud of you," Mrs. Best whispered thickly. "So very, very proud."

Daniel, not caring if his love for her showed plainly on his face, said, "That was an almighty undertaking, Belle."

"And she didn't miss one word," Jojo boasted.

Mr. Best said, "Belle, I want you to recite that at the next rally."

"Really?"

"Yes, ma'am."

Belle looked to Daniel and his smile met her own. Could she really stand in front of a crowd and recite Miss Watkins's famous poem? Belle never imagined herself speaking from behind a podium like she'd seen Daniel and Mrs. Best do, but maybe she could. Now that she was free and literate, maybe she could do anything she desired in this new, free world. For Belle Palmer, life was wonderful, and it was made even more so because of all the people she loved.

During the second week of September, a big box was delivered to the Best house by one of the local express companies. It was for Belle. Hoping and praying it would contain her new Singer sewing machine, Belle proudly signed her name on the receipt and the driver went on his way.

"Is that the sewing machine?" Jo asked excitedly.

"I don't know." An equally excited Belle quickly searched the box's exterior for a marking that might answer the question. When her eyes came across the words *I. M. Singer and Company,* she jumped for joy. "This is it, Jo! It's my sewing machine! Run tell the papas we need a crowbar. Something to open this thing with."

Jojo took off.

She returned a few minutes later with the papas, as she and Belle had taken to calling their fathers. Daniel and Mrs. Best also came in response to hearing of Belle's good news.

Both fathers went at the big box with their crowbars, and moments later they were lifting out Belle's spanking-new sewing machine. She fell in love from the moment she saw it. It was black, had a swanlike neck and was mounted on a short cabinet made to sit at. There were three small drawers down the cabinet's front that would hold threads and other notions perfectly.

While everyone looked on, smiling, Belle dug down in the box and found the detailed instructions promised in the advertisement. She experienced an even greater joy as she scanned the words on the cover with ease. The ability to read was truly a blessing.

"It says that the machine makes something called a lock stitch—"

For the rest of the afternoon, Belle sat in the center of the floor, reading her manual and looking over her machine. No one bothered her. The members of her family did peek in on her every now and again, but Belle was so engrossed they doubted she even noticed.

That evening after dinner, Daniel gathered his courage and asked the papas if he and Belle could go walking.

"How far?" James Palmer asked.

"Just up the road, sir. We won't be gone long."

"Take your sister," his father said.

Daniel almost protested, but knew if he did, he and Belle might not get to go walking at all. "Yes, sir."

The papas smiled fatherly.

Daniel went to find Josephine.

Daniel paid Jo five cents to walk on the opposite side of the road and a ways behind.

Jojo looked up at him. "Sure, I'll stay out of the way, but I want fifty cents next time."

"Fifty cents?!"

She nodded. "I love you both, but if the papas find out you bribed me to look the other way, five cents isn't going to be enough for all the trouble we'll be in."

Belle thought she had a point. Belle also thought Daniel was right: Jojo was a pest. Sometimes.

Daniel told his sister, "You're going to be in love one day, and I hope you won't need my help because I'm going to charge you five dollars."

Jo didn't seem impressed as she stuck out her palm for her payment. Daniel put the coins in her hand.

"Thanks," she told him with a smile.

He grouched back, "Be thankful I don't leave you tied to a tree and pick you up on the way home."

A smiling Belle took his hand. "Come on. We have to be back soon, remember?"

Daniel did and so let Belle lead him down the road.

They walked a ways in silence and basked in their semi-privacy and in the presence of each other.

Daniel said, "Did I tell you that your father asked me about my intentions toward you?"

"No. Did he?"

Daniel nodded.

"What did you say?"

"That I wanted to marry you and love you for the rest of my life."

A very moved Belle stopped and looked up into his eyes. "I want to marry you and love you for the rest of my life, too."

The kiss that followed cemented their words. When it ended, Daniel held her close to his heart and whispered against her hair, "And one day, I want to give you rubies and sapphires and a big old house—"

Belle thrilled at his words, but she didn't need jewels, only him. "I love you, Daniel Best."

He looked down at her with his heart in his eyes and declared, "I love you, too, Miss Belle."

epilogue

"For heaven's sake, Belle, sit still or you'll be the only bride wearing a curling-iron imprint on her cheek."

Jojo was working on Belle's hair and having the hardest time.

"I'm sorry," Belle offered apologetically. "But I'm so happy I could dance a jig. Wait until you get married. You'll see."

"Not if it makes me so addled I forget how it feels to be burned by a hot hair iron."

Mrs. Best, seated on the edge of Belle's bed, smiled at the dry wit of her youngest.

Jojo set the iron onto the lip of the small brazier and critically assessed her work. Belle's hair had grown out long enough for it to be brushed up and styled into a fashionable topknot. "You look beautiful."

Belle picked up the hand mirror. The face she saw reflected in the glass bore very little resemblance to the dirty, exhausted and terrified young woman she'd been the day Daniel coaxed her out of the ditch. Staring back were the confident features of a woman who was loved and intelligent, mistress of her own business and, yes, soon to be Daniel's wife. She smiled up into the black eyes of the young girl who'd been a sister to her in every way. "You did a grand job, Jo."

"I think she did, as well," Mrs. Best added sincerely.

"As Papa always says, it helps to start with a good foundation."

Mrs. Best nodded an agreement. "Now, let's get her into her dress."

Once the dress was on, Belle felt like a princess. The ivory-colored, high-collared gown had been lovingly made by her own hand. The hooped slip beneath gave the skirt just the right amount of volume, and the lace trim Mrs. Best had sent for all the way to Spain added to its beauty. "Do you think Daniel will like it?"

"My brother would have to be blind not to."

"It's magnificent, Belle," Mrs. Best concurred. "Every stitch is perfection."

"I'm so nervous. I can't believe he loves me."

"Everyone loves you," Jojo told her. "Well, maybe not Francine, but she doesn't count."

Both Best women came up behind Belle, and they were all reflected in the tall, mahogany stand-up mirror.

Jo asked, "If I somehow get addled enough to want to marry, will you make me a dress as grand as this?"

"Even grander, if you wish." Belle thought back to all she'd been through since escaping slavery last year and tears filled her eyes. "How can I ever thank you two for all you've done?" She hugged them both with a fierceness that reflected her love and gratitude.

"Stop crying," Jojo admonished affectionately. "That's Mama's job."

"Yes, it is," Cecilia pointed out, wiping at her own tears with a lacy monogrammed handkerchief. "This is going to be a three-handkerchief day, I just know it."

"I'm just so happy," Belle crowed.

Jojo took her by the hand. "Come on. Let's get you to your papa before you and Mama flood the room."

Mr. Palmer was waiting outside the door to escort her down to the parlor. Once Cecilia and Jojo left Belle alone with him, his eyes were wet, as well. "I wish your mother was here to see you."

"Me, too, Papa." Belle gave him a hug. Having her mama there would have made the day even more spectacular, but the Vigilance Committee was still searching and Belle prayed every night that good news was forthcoming.

"Are you ready?" he asked.

Belle smiled like the happy young woman that she was. "Yes, Papa, I am."

He held out his arm, she put her hand lightly upon it and let him lead her down to the parlor.

Downstairs, Daniel stood in the parlor flanked by his parents and the Morgan brothers, who'd come back to town to stand up with him. Also in attendance were a few other Whittaker residents, including the Reverend and Bea Meldrum. Daniel was glad they'd come and he was doing his best not to show how antsy he felt inside, but it was difficult. He and Belle were about to be married and his happy heart was threatening to burst through the seams of his new brown suit. A year had passed since he'd declared his intentions to her father, and although he'd thought this day would never arrive, it had. He was so grateful for her love. He'd probably be married to Francine if Belle had not come into his life, a realization that made him shudder. But Francine and her baby were in Indiana with an aunt, and he was awaiting the appearance of the young lady he planned to cherish for the rest of his life.

Belle entered the parlor on the arm of her father and Daniel couldn't take his eyes off her. From her lacy ivory dress and matching high-button shoes to the ivory ribbon framing her hair, she was stunning. The Morgans were grinning, his father was beaming and his mother's handkerchief was already sodden with joyful tears.

Belle and her father crossed the parlor to Daniel's side. Once they were all positioned, the reverend opened his Bible and asked, "Who gives this woman?"

Mr. Palmer answered in a proud and strong voice, "Her mother and I." He placed a solemn kiss on Belle's brow and stepped aside. Daniel took her hand in his and the short ceremony began.

Under the reverend's guidance they spoke their vows, and everyone in the room could see the love in the couple's eyes. Daniel slipped the small gold ring onto her finger and Belle was so moved, she just knew she was going to shake apart into a thousand jubilant pieces.

The reverend intoned to those in attendance, "What God has brought together let no man put asunder." He then smiled kindly at the two young people and declared,

"Daniel and Belle, I now pronounce you man and wife. Daniel, you may kiss your bride."

As everyone applauded, he took Belle into his arms and their kiss sealed a love that would last forever.

AUTHOR'S NOTE

I hope you enjoyed Belle and Daniel's story. After its first publication, many readers both young and old wanted to know if Belle and Daniel actually married, so I took that into consideration this time around. All of the historical elements of Belle's story are well-documented, from the terrible mandates of the Fugitive Slave Act of 1850, to the pay-on-time arrangements offered by the Singer Sewing Machine Company. Even the book Jojo complained about reading (because it was written by a man) was a text read by young women of that era. If this book has made you curious about other historical aspects of Belle's story, here are the sources I used to make Belle's story come alive. Look for them in your public library.

Blockson, Charles L. *Hippocrene Guide to the Underground Railroad,* New York: Hippocrene Books, 1994.

Bennett, Lerone, Jr. *Before the Mayflower: A History of Black America,* New York: Penguin Books/Johnson Publishing, 1987.

Litwak, Leon F. *North of Slavery: The Negro in the Free States, 1790–1860.* Chicago: University of Chicago Press, 1961.

Quarles, Benjamin. *Black Abolitionists,* New York: Oxford University Press, 1972.

Sterling, Dorothy A. *We Are Your Sisters: Black Women in the Nineteenth Century,* New York: Doubleday, 1976.

In closing, I'd like to say thanks to Linda Gill and Glenda Howard at Harlequin Books for their faith, help and support in bringing Belle's story back to life. I will be forever grateful. Thanks also to Ms. LaToya Hopkins-Kimbrough for her teacher's touch on the discussion questions. I'm sure her students at Brunswick Elementary in Gary, Indiana, will be impressed to see her name in print. Last but not least, a big thank-you to my readers, because without you there would be no Beverly Jenkins. Keep reading, everybody, and look for Jojo's story next! Love you all. B.

QUESTIONS FOR DISCUSSION

1. What do you know about African-American history that you didn't know before reading Belle's story?

2. Were there free black communities in your area before the Civil War? How would you go about finding out?

3. Why do you think it was so important for Daniel that he honour the promise he had made to Francine's dying mother, even though he was beginning to question his feelings for Francine and was developing feelings for Belle?

4. Why do you think it took humiliation at the hands of Francine at the picnic to motivate Belle to learn to read and not the initial talk she had with Mrs. Best on the same subject?

5. Do you think education is important now as it was in Belle's time? If yes, why? If no, why not?

6. Had Belle not come into Daniel's life, would his eyes ever have opened to the real Francine the Queen everyone else saw?

7. Why do you think the kidnapping experience by the slave catchers changed the Morgan brothers' outlook on life so dramatically?

8. Was the threat of losing Daniel the only reason Francine seemed so determined to break Belle's spirit?

9. If you could start your own business the way Belle did, what type of business would it be?

10. Did you enjoy the story? If yes, why? If no, why not?